I know what you must be thinking. If I can happily tolerate a New Age hippy for a mother, how can I possibly be embarrassed by a disco-dancing father with a hole in the elbow of his cardigan? Let me explain. Eleanor Sharratt is horribly conventional and terrified of what her friends might think or say. She likes her parents to be anonymous, silent and preferably invisible. But Nel Sharpe is a different kind of girl altogether. She looks like an elegant, fantastical bird and she doesn't give a damn about what anybody else thinks.

www.**kids**at**random**om**house**.co.uk

JUGGLING LESSONS

JUGGLING LESSONS
A CORGI BOOK 0552 547956

Published in Great Britain by Corgi Books,
an imprint of Random House Children's Books

This edition published 2002

1 3 5 7 9 10 8 6 4 2

Papers used by Random House Children's Books are natural, recyclable
products made from wood grown in sustainable forests. The manufacturing
processes conform to the environmental regulations of the country of origin.

Set in 12/14½pt Bembo by
Falcon Oast Graphic Art Ltd, East Hoathly, East Sussex

Corgi Books are published by Random House Children's Books
61–63 Uxbridge Road, London W5 5SA
a division of The Random House Group Ltd,
in Australia by Random House Australia (Pty) Ltd,
20 Alfred Street, Milsons Point, Sydney, NSW 2061, Australia
in New Zealand by Random House New Zealand Ltd,
18 Poland Road, Glenfield, Auckland 10, New Zealand
and in South Africa by Random House (Pty) Ltd,
Endulini, 5A Jubilee Road, Parktown 2193, South Africa

THE RANDOM HOUSE GROUP Limited Reg. No. 954009

A CIP catalogue record for this book is available from the British Library.

Printed and bound in Great Britain by
Bookmarque Ltd, Croydon, Surrey

Juggling Lessons

Jan Page

CORGI BOOKS

For Emma

CHAPTER ONE

If you met me today, I would tell you my name was Eleanor Sharratt. You would see a tall, slim girl with long blonde hair tied back in a neat ponytail. On closer inspection you would realize that almost everything about me is long – long hair, long legs, long fingers, a long straight nose . . . I even have long toes. It's as if I've been grabbed by my hands and feet, and stretched. I expect you would judge that my eyes are my best feature – large and blue like a baby doll. And if I happened to be wearing mascara you might think that my curly, long (there's that word again) eyelashes were false. All in all, you would probably conclude that Eleanor Sharratt looks like a long thin stick.

I don't think you'd find Eleanor Sharratt very interesting. *I* certainly don't. Recently she has become very quiet. Ever since she had her brace fitted she has only opened her mouth when absolutely necessary. She nibbles her food. When she has to ask for something she mumbles and is made to repeat it. Eleanor always gives the shortest reply to any question. 'How are you getting on at school?' 'Fine.' 'Have you done your homework?' 'Yes.' To say 'no' would only prolong the conversation.

At this precise moment I am looking at Eleanor Sharratt in the bedroom mirror. She is removing some 'disgusting' blue nail varnish from each of her long toenails. Her father and stepmother have just spent ten minutes debating whether or not blue nail varnish is 'appropriate' for a thirteen-year-old girl to wear. Eleanor considered joining in, but as this would have involved opening her mouth, she simply sat and let them get on with it. When the decision was made, she raised her large blue eyes to the ceiling and heaved an irritated sigh. Then she rose slowly from the sofa and dragged herself upstairs, shutting the door loudly, but not loudly enough as to be accused of slamming it. I wish Eleanor had more fighting spirit – I wish she would shout and scream and stand up for the rights of blue nail varnish. But she can't be bothered. She just reaches for the remover and stares at her strange long limbs in the mirror.

Downstairs, Dad and Julie are getting on each other's nerves. Julie is washing up noisily and Dad is telling her to sit down and put her feet up. Julie is pregnant, so soon I'll have a brother or sister. Technically, this will be a 'half-brother or -sister' but Dad doesn't like that description – 'Which half?' he says. 'Left or right, top or bottom?' He doesn't like 'stepmum' either, but Julie is only twenty-four, so nobody ever mistakes her for my real mother. They usually think she's the babysitter. Actually she *was* the babysitter, which was how she met Dad in the first place.

Dad is being told for the tenth time this week that he 'doesn't understand what it's like to be pregnant'. I can hear it all through the floor of my room, which is right above the kitchen. I hear lots of conversations that way. Things I would rather not hear. Like Julie moaning about 'Eleanor's mother'. I know they have rude nick-names for her – that they think she ought to 'grow up' and 'face her responsibilities'. Julie complains that Fizz sends silly presents, but never buys me school uniform or sensible shoes. Dad says Fizz was the 'biggest mistake of his life'. I can only imagine, as I arrange the straps of my skimpy new dress, that I must be Dad's *longest* mistake, a tall thin disaster, stretching out over the past thirteen years.

Let's not get too depressed. Tomorrow at 3 p.m. (if Fizz is on time, which she usually isn't) I will transform into somebody completely different, somebody far more interesting and exciting! But today's not over yet. I've got to get through the school disco first.

Why am I not looking forward to the school disco? After all, it's summer, and the end of the school year. I have a new dress that Dad disapproves of – always a good sign. And for once I have no spots on my back. Most importantly, I know for a fact that Craig Basford is going to be there – he was spotted buying a ticket yesterday lunchtime. Craig Basford is not only the most gorgeous boy in Year 8, he is actually taller than me. I have it on good authority – from Hannah, who saw him looking at me in PE – that he fancies me. Tonight could be the night.

So why have I lost all enthusiasm for the school disco? Because my stupid father filled in a reply slip saying he would be a parent supervisor.

'Time to go!' Dad has just shouted up the stairs, using

his jolly 'let's forget about the nail varnish incident' voice. I catch myself mouthing a foul reply at the mirror. I used to be such a sweet little girl . . .

'Eleanor! Are you coming or not?'

I slip into my shoes and trudge downstairs.

I discover, to my relief, that Dad has been put on the ticket desk in the entrance hall. If he'd been given the job of separating snoggers, I would have died. I couldn't bear to be disentangled from Craig Basford by my own father! But I'm jumping the gun here. Who's to say I'm going to be snogging anyone tonight? I've never had a proper kiss and I've no idea how to do it. I've been practising on my pillow, as advised in my magazine, but as pillows don't have teeth or noses to bang into, I'm none the wiser. There's also the problem of my brace. I should be comforted by the fact that Craig Basford has one too, but what if there's a loud clang as we meet? What if our braces get caught up and we can't tear ourselves apart?

Speaking of Craig Basford, he has just walked in! He's wearing a black Ralph Lauren top and combat trousers. As he walks past me, I get a strong whiff of expensive deodorant, or is it aftershave? Hannah and I make a dash for the loo to re-curl our eyelashes and plan my first move.

There's never much to say about the disco itself. We spend weeks working ourselves into a frenzy of excitement, and when it actually happens it's always rather boring and uneventful. The girls dance in small circles, while the boys hang around the sides of the school hall.

12

As most thirteen-year-old boys' idea of fashion is a football shirt, it looks as if they're watching a match, mostly supporting Man United. After half a dozen dances (which should be enough to give the impression that we're not *that* interested in boys) Hannah and I decide it's time to bump into Craig, who has just walked out in the direction of the canteen.

'The Coke's warm,' says Craig, looking me straight in the eyes.

For once Eleanor Sharratt feels a spark of enthusiasm, a knot of excitement clenching in her stomach. 'Yeah,' I mutter. 'Rubbish, isn't it.'

'He's so going to ask you to dance!' Hannah insists, as we go to the loo yet again to apply more lip-gloss. For once, I believe her. All the signs are good. I hope he waits till the slow dances at the end of the evening. It's so much more romantic than jiggling about two metres away from each other and there's more chance of a kiss!

We follow Craig back into the hall to be met by a very strange sight. For some strange reason the DJ has just announced that it's time for a parents and teachers dance.

'Help!' I whisper to Hannah. 'We've got to get Dad out of here before he hears about it.' But we're too late. He has just bounded into the room and joined the bunch of forty-year-olds who are jerking their flabby bodies in time to some awful seventies disco hit. Most of us suffering from Embarrassing Parents syndrome take on the nonchalant air of orphans. In my case, this turns out to be a fatal error of judgement. If I had had any sense, I would have dragged my father off the dance floor *before* he began his impression of John Travolta in

Saturday Night Fever.

I can hardly bear to tell you what happens next . . . Dad wiggles his hips and points his right finger in the air. This is followed by several twirls and what can only be described as a silly walk. Then he picks up Miss Biggs, my physics teacher, and spins her round the room as if they are a couple of ice-dancers! I should point out that Miss Biggs eats a jam doughnut every break time and has consequently lost her centre of gravity. Dad has just sent her flying and she's landed on her knees with a crack we could hear above the music!

This is a nightmare – I don't know what to do. I can't stand for this to go on a moment longer, but to drag him away would reveal that he's my father. Why won't anybody else stop him? But no, they're doing the opposite! The other parents and teachers have gathered at the side and are letting him have the floor to himself. Craig Basford has joined the crowd of lads who are clapping and cheering, and most of the girls are in hysterics of laughter. I just want to die.

'I'm going to write to *Kiss* magazine,' I mutter to Hannah. '"My Most Embarrassing Moment". If they publish it you get ten pounds.'

'They give twenty pounds to the "My Most Embarrassing Moment of the Month",' she adds.

'I'd get that, no problem. I could win the "My Most Embarrassing Moment of the Year" – of the century.'

'Of the millennium!' Hannah shrieks.

'It's all right for you, he's not your father . . .' Now he's doing a mock bull-fighting routine with a paper napkin. 'There's no way Craig will ask me to dance now.'

'But Craig doesn't know that that's your dad,' replies Hannah, just a moment too soon.

'A-a-a-a, staying alive, staying alive,' sings Dad as he runs into the crowd and makes a grab for my wrist!

'Come on, Eleanor, let's do the tango!'

'No way! Stop doing that!'

'Stop doing what? This?' he laughs, spinning around with his arms in the air, revealing two large holes in the elbows of his cardigan.

'You're really embarrassing me!'

'I'm only having a bit of fun!' At last the wretched song comes to an end. Dad spins to a dramatic halt and bows to the applauding crowd. For the first time in my life I consider committing murder.

You won't be surprised to learn that I didn't speak to Dad for the rest of the evening. The slow dances came and went. A couple of nerdy boys asked me to dance, but I said 'no' because I was still hoping Craig was going to ask me. Of course he didn't. Not even after Hannah went and told him I was adopted.

'I can't wait to get out of this dump,' I tell Hannah as we take refuge in the toilets. The disco's nearly over and we seem to have spent more time in here than in the hall. 'Six whole weeks of freedom.'

Hannah purses her lips. 'Don't say that . . . I'll miss you.'

'Thanks.' I'm very fond of Hannah, but I can't bring myself to say, 'Me too.'

Dad just doesn't seem to realize that I'm furious with him. He thinks he's been the highlight of the evening. He's been humming away and tapping out his dance steps on the steering wheel all the way home. 'I bet you didn't know I could dance,' he says excitedly.

'I still don't. What's got into you? You never do that sort of thing!' I'm so angry I've managed a reply of three sentences.

'Ah, you'd be surprised the sort of things I used to do,' he sighs.

'Fizz would never embarrass me in that way.'

'Your mother's a circus performer, for God's sake! What could be more embarrassing than that?'

There's a long silence between us, each of us locked into our own thoughts. I'm thinking about the weeks that lie ahead – things I've scarcely dared to imagine. In case something went wrong. In case Fizz got an engagement abroad and couldn't take me. But now there are only seventeen hours to go. I can feel the twitchings under my skin – the hard outer shell of Eleanor Sharratt is about to smash to make way for a new, colourful and – dare I say? - beautiful creature.

So if you meet me after 3 p.m. tomorrow, I will tell you my name is Nel Sharpe, talented tumbler and juggler, and daughter of the one and only Flying Fizz.

CHAPTER TWO

It is 3.45 p.m. and, surprise, surprise, the magical transformation has not yet taken place. Dad and I are sitting at our usual table overlooking the car park of the motorway service station. Fizz is forty-five minutes late, which is irritating, but still an hour short of her record.

Fizz — she is not the type of person you'd ever call Mum — lives on the edge of a small fishing village in Cornwall. Dad and Julie (whom I never call Mum for other reasons) live in the Midlands, just outside Derby, which is about as far from the sea as you can possibly get. I realize I have left myself out of this equation. If you walked up to me now and asked me for my address, I don't know which one I would give. Because at this precise moment I am neither Eleanor Sharratt nor Nel Sharpe — just a grey blob of teenage matter. Waiting . . .

Dad and Fizz refuse to come to each other's houses, so they each drive halfway and meet at a service station. When I say 'meet' I do not mean that they actually come into contact with each other. Believe it or not, my parents have neither seen nor spoken to each other for the past eight years. Since I was five I have been the negotiator in this war and, unfortunately, neither side is interested in peace. When I was younger I thought it was a bit strange, now I think it's pathetic. Can they really hate each other that much? They're meant to be the adults, but sometimes I feel more grown up than they are.

After breakfast Dad packs the car and checks the pressure in the tyres. Julie drags herself out of bed at the last moment and gives me an awkward hug on the doorstep. She says, 'We'll miss you,' and I nod. Julie is not an outright liar. She *will* miss me – meaning she will notice that I am not around. As soon as she hears the car turn the corner, she probably heaves a huge sigh of relief. She will have Dad all to herself for the next six weeks. They can discuss baby names and decorate the spare bedroom and do whatever grown-ups do when they're left alone. I don't want to think about it.

We arrive at the service station early and reconnoitre the car park. Luckily, Fizz has a very distinctive car. There is no pink and white striped Volvo, so Dad knows he is safe. We establish our lookout point at a table by the window of the self-service restaurant. Dad insists that I order steak and kidney pie or roast beef – something defiantly meaty. Fizz is a vegetarian, so he wants me to stock up on some protein. In fact, he refers to her as a 'bloody vegetarian', which I find rather strange. If there's one thing vegetarians aren't, it's bloody.

After lunch we maintain our stake-out position in the restaurant, despite an elderly waiter's attempt to shift us. Dad camouflages himself behind a copy of the *Saturday Telegraph*, while I am put on afternoon watch. Dad refuses to undertake this duty himself. As the moment of

Fizz's possible arrival draws near, he will not risk even a glimpse of her wacky painted Volvo. He seems to think it will contaminate him.

I know that when I say, 'She's here!' Dad will leap from his seat, blow me a kiss and run to hide in the shop. It's usually such a funny sight that I'm tempted to give false alarms. I imagine him squeezing beneath the racks of teenage magazines, or burrowing under the mountains of pick'n'mix. One hot summer's day Fizz will walk into that shop to buy an ice cream. She'll open the lid of the freezer and find him shivering amongst the Magnums and Cornettos. Then they'll *have* to meet. But this will never happen. Fizz knows where he hides and walks straight past.

But she's not here yet! I do wish she wouldn't do this to me . . .

Fizz is always late and always blames it on the 'bloody tourist traffic'. It makes me think of multiple pile-ups on the M5 – cars full of people in colourful shirts and straw hats, their dead bodies smeared with blood. But then I've always had a lurid imagination. This frequent use of the word 'bloody' is just about the only thing Dad and Fizz have in common. They don't realize this, of course, and if I told them, they would stop using the word instantly.

Dad knows she does it deliberately. He claims that *artistes* – this word is said with a sneering French accent – are always late because they think it's the sign of a creative mind. I happen to know that Fizz is never late for a performance – only for hand-overs. The longer Dad spends fretting in the motorway restaurant, the more satisfaction she gets. His punishment is to suffer three hours of artificial plants, soft music and disappointing cream cakes. His crime? Just being him.

When my parents first split up, Dad told me I was a princess because I was going to have two homes. Even at the age of five I knew princesses did not live in terraced houses, but I suppose it was a comforting thought. He and Fizz bought places a few miles from each other and I spent a week with each parent. To save carting everything back and forth, I had two sets of clothes, two tricycles and two pairs of wellington boots. Lucky, lucky me. Then Fizz announced she was going to Paris to train as a mime artist – sorry, *artiste*. I stopped being a member of the royal family and found myself with just one home, and one parent. Fizz embarked on a mission to discover herself and Dad discovered he was in love with my babysitter. That was when all communication between them stopped.

When Fizz finally returned to England it was to live in a remote cottage on the Cornish cliffs. In Dad's eyes, I don't have a home in Cornwall, I simply 'visit' my mother's place. But he has never been there. He has never climbed the narrow stairs and entered my tiny bedroom, never sat on the narrow bed and gazed out of the window at the triangle of sea – its colour constantly shifting between green and blue. He has never lain there in the dark, watching the stars and listening to the waves beating time against the rocks. He has never had breakfast in a cave, or lit a bonfire on the beach, or swum in the pouring rain. And I hope he never does. Because then he would meet Nel, my other self. A different child in strange clothes, dancing in the rock pools – feeling at home not just in her tiny bedroom, but in the great universe itself.

Enough of the poetry. 'She's here!'

Dad goes into action. He throws down his newspaper, kisses me roughly on the head and disappears through the restaurant doors as fast as a member of the emergency services. It's not a very pleasant way to say goodbye, but I'm used to it.

'Darling!' It's thirty seconds later, and Fizz is running into the restaurant. She narrowly avoids colliding with an elderly man carrying a tray of fish and chips. He makes tutting sounds in her direction. No doubt he thinks she's a gypsy – or one of those homeless people with a dog, a penny whistle and a pile of *Big Issue*s. She does look extraordinary. She has dyed her hair purple and let it form fat dreadlocks, which tumble down her back. She is wearing a long dress with fringes round the bottom and a pair of jangling leather sandals. On her right arm she has a henna tattoo and there is a tiny diamond stud twinkling in her nose.

'Nel! It's so wonderful to see you! I've missed you like mad.'

'Me too . . .' Fizz hugs me so tightly I feel I'm going to suffocate in her petunia oil perfume. 'You're so late. I was starting to worry.'

'Sorry, darling, not my fault. I could murder a cup of coffee. Do you want anything?'

'No thanks.'

I know what you must be thinking. If I can happily tolerate a New Age hippy for a mother, how can I possibly be embarrassed by a disco-dancing father with a hole in the elbow of his cardigan? Let me explain. Eleanor Sharratt is horribly conventional and terrified of what her friends might think or say. She likes her parents to be anonymous, silent and preferably invisible. But Nel Sharpe is a different kind of girl altogether.

She is still a long, thin stick, of course, but she relishes her shape. She may even exaggerate it. To her long list of 'long' attributes she will add dangly earrings, long velvety scarves and long swirly skirts. Tonight, Fizz will plait her hair into hundreds of long thin strands, each secured with a coloured bead. She will paint every long toenail a different colour if she feels so inclined, and put rings on every long finger. Nel Sharpe looks like an elegant, fantastical bird and she doesn't give a damn about what anybody else thinks.

Fizz comes back to the table with a bottle of flavoured mineral water and a piece of flapjack. 'I decided against the coffee. It makes my hands shake,' she explains.

Obviously, this is not good if you earn your living throwing strange objects into the air. Fizz tells me that her latest speciality is juggling exotic fruit. It's easy to juggle oranges and apples, of course. But try juggling a pineapple, a lemon and a banana! It's not the awkward shapes that are the problem, it's the difference in their weight. She discovered her skill a few months ago when she decided to go on a fruit only diet. To purify her system. 'I feel fantastic and I've got a whole new show!' she announces.

Fizz sits back in the plastic chair and closes her eyes. She takes several deep breaths. I think she's trying to 'slip a second' – it's a yoga thing she does. If you can manage not to think for a whole second, it gives you eight hours of extra energy. Or something like that.

'Can we go now? Only I've been here since three o'clock and I'm beginning to take root.' How easily I speak when I'm Nel – the phrases and sentences cascade out of my mouth like a fountain. I instantly feel more confident and assertive. The dental brace is no longer a restraining device – it's an ornament. I smile and let it flash in the afternoon sun.

'I'm sorry, darling, of course. It's hideous here. No natural materials – everything's plastic. I can feel waves of negative energy.' My mother is completely bonkers, but I love her to bits.

Actually, I suspect the negative waves are coming from my poor father. I've just spotted him creeping into the car park. He glances around furtively, fumbling with his keys as he attempts to get back into his car. He starts the engine immediately and screeches out of his parking space. The man watching the security cameras probably thinks he's a car-thief. I breathe a sigh of relief. Mission accomplished. In the way of all Hollywood disaster movies, the deadly missiles have not run into each other and the End of the World has been averted yet again.

CHAPTER THREE

Cows' bottoms. That is what we are staring at – about fifty cows' bottoms, strolling slowly down the narrow lane, flicking their tails from side to side as they fend off imaginary flies. I've wound up the window and I'm pinching my nostrils together, but it makes no difference whatsoever. 'They stink.'

'It's a country smell,' replies Fizz, as if that makes it all right.

'I don't care, it's disgusting!'

Guess what, I've discovered that the flies aren't imaginary at all – just so small that they're barely visible to the naked eye. A gang of them has invaded the car because Fizz refused to wind her window up. Now they've found a mouldy jam tart on the back seat. Great.

It has to be said, Fizz's car is a tip. I wouldn't be surprised if she had mice nesting in it. The floor is littered with newspapers, chocolate wrappers and hard brown banana skins. Surprisingly, she hates people dropping litter. She confronts lads who drop beer cans into Trewyss harbour, or families who leave the remains of their picnic on the beach. 'Take it home with you!' she shouts. Only she never takes her litter home. She just leaves it in

Daisy – to fester and rot and become a breeding ground for flies.

We're only a few miles from the cottage, but this part of the journey seems to take for ever. The sea is playing hide and seek with us behind the tall hedgerows. Every so often there is a gap and I peer through a gate, trying to catch a glimpse of her as she skips between the hills. But she can't hide for ever. The lane narrows and narrows until it turns into the dirt track that leads onto the cliffs. Suddenly she's there, the beautiful Atlantic Ocean – stretching out her arms like a long-lost aunt, waiting to give me an enormous wet kiss.

At last, we've arrived!

Fizz's cottage is behind a cornfield that goes right up to the cliff path. It's a small, dirty-white house with tiny windows and flaking blue paintwork. The front door has been stuck for as long as I can remember, so we always go round the back. There was probably a garden once, with a lawn and flowerbeds; now it's a mass of tangled weeds and windswept heathers. The front is just a worn patch of grass and gravel, a car park for Daisy and a campsite for any visiting friends.

I love being at the cottage. I like the fact that I don't have to wipe my feet on the doormat, or remove my shoes and arrange them neatly on the shoe-rack. It's such a relief not to have to wear my Marks and Spencer's slippers or hang up my coat ('On the peg, please, Eleanor, not over the end of the banisters'). Who cares if dinner isn't on the table promptly at six, or that some days there will be nothing to eat but cornflakes because Fizz has forgotten to go shopping? I'm never told when to go to bed, so sometimes I go at midnight, and sometimes at half-past eight. Fizz never forbids to me watch certain television programmes because 'they're not suitable'. (Actually, the reason for this is that she doesn't have a television, but if she *did* have one, I'm sure I'd be allowed to watch whatever I liked.)   Apart from missing my favourite American sitcom, life here is bliss.

'Let's go into Trewyss and raid the chip shop,' announces Fizz, juggling casually with three satsumas she's found lurking in the fruit bowl. 'I could do with a walk.'

Am I made to unpack first, so that all my clothes don't get creased? No. Am I made to put on a jumper in case the weather turns chilly? No. Am I forced to go to the loo because it's a long walk to the harbour and I don't want the embarrassment of having to pee in the fields? Of course not. But I *do* change – making a quick dash up to my room, which is just the same as I left it three months ago (only dustier), leaping out of my jeans and swiftly wrapping a tie-dye sarong round my waist.

'How's your juggling practice?' asks Fizz, as we stride up a hill on the other side of the bay. She's a lot fitter than me and doesn't seem to have noticed that I'm wheezing three paces behind.

'I haven't done any for ages. You know what it's like. If I even mention the word "circus", they go all quiet and peculiar on me.'

'Pathetic . . . ' Fizz heaves a big sigh, hands on hips, and then leaps over a stile. 'Ah well, you'll get plenty of practice this summer. I've got heaps of bookings. You can be my "lovely assistant"!'

'I can't wait!'

There are a few moments of silence. I know what Fizz is thinking. She is remembering the days when I used to join the circus parades on my tiny unicycle, a skinny eight-year-old wearing a stripy leotard and a yellow net tutu skirt. I learnt to juggle with three beanbags and Fizz taught me to do perfect cartwheels. I was everybody's darling – little Nel, Fizz's girl, who popped up in the holidays and then vanished without a trace.

'Anyway,' Fizz continues, talking to the ocean rather than me, 'Los Diabolos will be here tomorrow. They're touring with us – it's going to be fantastic!'

'Los Diabolos? Have I met them before?'

Fizz shakes her head. 'No, I came across them at Easter, when I was in Spain. They're an acrobatic stunt group from Barcelona. Their show is amazing! It's a family business – Rosa and Dídac, and their son Oriol. Oh, yes, and Jordi of course – Dídac's twin brother: they look identical and it all gets very confusing! The men don't speak any English, apart from Oriol, who's been learning at school. Rosa's English is pretty good, but her accent is so strong I can hardly understand her. It's going to be great fun – you'll love them!'

OK, let's admit it. At the mention of the word 'son' my mind has switched instantly into Boy Mode. What if he's drop-dead gorgeous, with jet-black hair, piercing blue eyes and a fabulous tan? Stop! I must control myself! All I know so far is that he's male. Knowing my luck, he'll be seven and I'll be expected to babysit. 'How old is their son?' I ask, trying to sound as casual as possible.

'Not sure . . . about fifteen I think – a bit older than

you,' replies Fizz, sounding equally casual. Has she twigged? Probably. Fizz is one of the few grown-ups I can imagine being thirteen. She must remember what it's like to have a glimmer of romance looming on the horizon.

Talking of the horizon, the sun is about to set. No matter how hungry we are, we just have to stop and gaze at it. It makes my mouth drop open. I can feel myself becoming all poetic.

The sun is a round gold brooch, pinned on a pink silk scarf, threaded with blue and orange.

See what I mean? Back to asking important questions as if I couldn't care less about the answer (basically, how long have I got to make myself look irresistible?): 'Er, when are they arriving?'

'Tomorrow lunchtime.'

'Will you be able to plait my hair tonight?'

'Yes, if you're not too tired.'

'I'm not tired at all.' I stifle a large yawn.

Fizz buys us each a vegetable spring roll from the Sea Shanty café and we share a polystyrene tray of chips. I don't point out that spring rolls are traditionally Chinese rather than Cornish, or that polystyrene trays destroy the ozone layer, because if there's one thing I've learnt over the years, it's that you don't argue with Fizz when she's hungry.

We sit and make rude comments about the passers by – the fat ones with wobbly thighs, the ginger-nuts with lobster faces, the families who all look the same as each other – tall, thin, hooked noses, glasses and mousy-coloured hair. Night falls, the coloured lights twinkle around the harbour, and the pubs fill to bursting. People spill onto the streets clutching mugs of beer, laughing and talking in their various regional accents. I could go on about the sights and smells of Trewyss, but I think that's enough local colour for one day.

It's ten o'clock and we're back at the cottage. Fizz has got halfway round my head, plaiting my blonde locks into long thin ropes, which she fastens with purple and blue beads. I hope Oriol goes for this look, or it's going to be a terrible waste of time. I suddenly feel utterly ashamed of myself. Why on earth did I think that? Definitely shades of Eleanor Sharratt creeping in here, sneakily, trying to take me unawares. I suppose I shouldn't be too hard on myself, I've only been Nel for a few hours. It's going to take some time to adjust, but I must calm down.

FOUR IMPORTANT POINTS TO REMEMBER
1. I wanted plaits long before I knew anything about some gorgeous Spanish fifteen-year-old coming for the summer, which proves that I am doing this for myself and not for some boy – so there!
2. Just because he's foreign, it does not automatically mean he's going to be gorgeous (this is very important, I must hold onto this idea).
3. This holiday is about being with my *mother* – spending Quality Time together. It is about developing that vital relationship and not about having a holiday romance with the first person who happens to turn up, even if he is Spanish and gorgeous (which he might not be).
4. However, if Oriol *does* turn out to be gorgeous, and

nice, it's going to be impossible not to fancy him, so why resist it? I could be about to fall in love (about time too, as I am fourteen in October).

Oh, I can't wait until tomorrow. Hannah could be in line to receive an extremely interesting postcard!

CHAPTER FOUR

A tatty old van towing a tiny caravan has just trundled up the path.

'It's Los Diabolos!' screams Fizz, bursting out of the cottage. '*Hola! Hola!*' The van draws to a halt and an amazingly beautiful woman is the first to leap out. She has a tangled mane of jet-black hair, huge dark brown eyes outlined in black pencil, a small bright red mouth and a superb slim figure. She's wearing tight black jeans, a black T-shirt and a black, silky bomber jacket. 'Rosa!' Fizz cries as they hug and kiss each other on both cheeks.

'Fantasteek!' Rosa laughs, pointing at the sea.

Fizz breaks into a stream of excited Spanish – I presume it's Spanish, it could be Japanese for all I know. A bleary-eyed man has got out now and is doing the same round of kisses. Which one of the twins is he? I wonder – Dídac or Jordi? Either way, he's short and slim, wearing a sleeveless vest, which reveals some rather impressive muscles and a very hairy chest! His hair is dark and thin, he has a long thin nose, a thick moustache, twinkling black eyes and a gold tooth. He reminds me of a bullfighter – he looks about as typically Spanish as you can imagine.

Now the other one has jumped out of the driving seat and is fetching a crate of wine from the van. He looks identical to his brother, just a bit fatter in the face. Jordi or Dídac (why doesn't Fizz introduce me?) plonks the crate down by the front door as if he's delivering our daily supply of milk and says something to Fizz in a gruff but musical voice. She immediately rushes indoors, nearly knocking me over in the process. She seems to have forgotten all about me. Or perhaps I've just become invisible.

But no. At last Rosa has spotted me lurking in the doorway. She steps forward and kisses me lightly on both cheeks. 'Please to meet you! I am Rosa.' I just love her accent, it's so very, very Spanish! The words clatter out – sharp, clipped, rhythmic – as if she's playing the castanets in her throat. 'This is Dídac, and he is Jordi.' So, Dídac is the thinner one doing stretching exercises on the clifftop, and Jordi is the driver who has just collapsed on the grass. That's all fine. But where is Oriol?

As you can imagine, I have spent the last three hours showering, shaving my legs and armpits, smothering myself with deodorant, applying a face pack, plucking my eyebrows, painting my nails, changing in and out of clothes, curling my eyelashes and putting on my make-up! So what's happened to the boy of my dreams? Has he decided to stay at home with his grandma? Or is this all just some sick joke of my mother's – perhaps he doesn't exist at all!

Then suddenly, as if she can read my mind, Rosa throws open the back doors of the van. And there he is, curled up, fast asleep on a pile of rugs, sighing and sucking his thumb, a set of long, curly, black lashes fluttering gently on his cheeks. Rosa shakes him and whispers in his ear. Oriol yawns, stretches to his full length, opens his eyes and looks around . . . Wow!

OK, where do I start? He has Rosa's eyes – large and dark. And he has Dídac's long, thin nose – or at least he will have by the time it's finished growing. His skin is smooth and brown, his hair dark and wavy. I wouldn't say he's absolutely perfect, but he beats Craig Basford by a million miles!

It turns out that Fizz has been searching for some wine glasses. Of course she hasn't got enough, not clean ones anyway. She emerges with one huge, beautiful goblet, which she hands to Rosa, a ludicrously tiny glass with a chipped gold rim, a pint beer glass, a plastic tumbler and what looks like the tooth mug from the bathroom. My thoughts immediately wander to Dad and Julie, who have entire sets of wine, champagne, whisky, sherry, brandy, beer, you-name-it-they-had-them-for-a-wedding-present glasses – all neatly on display in a large glass cabinet. But the Spaniards don't seem to care. Jordi opens the first bottle with a flourish and pours. He hands me the tooth mug, full of deep red wine. I take it and steal a glance at Fizz. Am I allowed? But I can't attract her attention. She's too busy chatting to Rosa. Dídac makes a long, dramatic toast in Spanish. Who knows what I'm wishing for, or celebrating, or supporting, or even denouncing? I swig it back and try to hide the fact that the wine tastes of toothpaste. If Dad knew I was drinking alcohol he'd have a fit!

So they're here – our constant companions for the next six weeks. Fizz and I will travel in Daisy, and Los Diabolos will follow us from festival to festival, up and down the county, with the odd foray into Devon, Somerset, or even Gloucestershire. If the weather's good, we'll camp. If it's not, we'll sleep in the car. I've a feeling that it's going to be 'fantasteek'!

It's two o'clock in the afternoon now and Fizz is drunk. She's not the only one – Rosa, Dídac and Jordi look fairly out of it too, sprawled across an old bedspread on the beach. Jordi, who apparently did most of the driving on the way over, is fast asleep. Dídac is lying with his head in Rosa's lap, staring at the clouds. Half a dozen empty red wine bottles roll around the blanket, clinking together like the wind chime in my bedroom. Nobody has had anything to eat, and I've got a headache.

And what is Oriol doing at this precise moment? He's standing at the water's edge, his jeans rolled up to his knees, staring at the waves. I want to walk down and start a conversation, but I can't speak Spanish and I've discovered that his English is pretty basic, despite what Fizz said about him learning it at school. All he's said so far has been 'Yes' and 'Pleeze' in a rather sexy accent!

The grown-ups are all dozing off in their drunken stupor while I'm sitting here like an idiot, all dressed up and nowhere to go. But I can't have a gorgeous Spaniard wandering around the beach, unsupervised! Any teenage holidaymaker could walk up and nab him for herself! Suddenly, my desire to talk to Oriol becomes a major emergency – I must get down there quickly. I run across the sand, jumping over holes and skirting sandcastles, picking up pace as I reach the wet flats, paying no attention to the streams of icy water, the sharp stones or the strange worm casts. By the time I reach Oriol my heart is pounding and I haven't a clue why I've come or what I'm going to say.

'Hola!' he says, smiling.

I presume this means 'hello', but I can't bring myself to reply in either language, so I grin back at him like a dork, and instantly regret revealing my brace. 'Do you like the sea?' I say idiotically.

'Yes. I like . . . big . . . the sea . . . go up and down.'

'You mean, the waves! Yes, we have big waves here. It's great for surfing.'

I can tell by the look on his face that he's already lost. 'Sorry?' he says appealingly.

'Surfing – surfboards.' I point at the lines of wet-suited bodies queuing hopefully in the sea. There is a long pause as we pretend to take great interest in their efforts to catch the waves.

'Ungreee!' Oriol says suddenly, as if he has been trying to remember the word for hours. He pats his stomach to make sure I've understood. At last we have something in common.

'Me too. Let's go and see what there is to eat in the cottage.' He looks blank, but I beckon him to follow and he does. Things are looking up.

Well, surprise, surprise, there is nothing to eat in the cottage, unless you count a tin of kidney beans and half a lemon. Oriol opens the cupboards and mutters. I can tell he's not impressed.

'Let's go to Trewyss and buy something,' I say several times, very slowly. I mime eating Sunday lunch, I act out buying a bar of chocolate and paying for it. I feel like I'm doing a drama lesson at school and it's making my mouth water.

At last he understands. He grabs an old duffel bag from the van and we set off on the cliff path. We walk in awkward silence, either because we don't know what to say or we don't know how. All I discover is that he smokes, which is not so good, and he is about a centimetre taller than me, which is great. I must remember to mention both facts to Hannah.

'Do you want a Cornish pasty?' I ask when we reach the harbour. Oriol shrugs. I might as well have asked him if he wanted boiled eyeballs and rabbit droppings. We join the queue outside the Traditional Cornish Pasty Shop. I wonder if people think Oriol is my boyfriend! I smile sweetly at him in the hope of adding to the illusion.

'How many years do you have?' he asks.

I think he wants to know my age. What should I reply? Thirteen sounds so babyish, and I look much older, especially with make-up on. I'm hesitating, pretending not to understand the question.

'Fifteen.' Oh my God, I've just lied. What if I'm found out? What if he checks with Fizz? I can feel myself blushing, I turn my face to the shop window and fix my gaze on the leek and Stilton pasties. What did I do that for? Why didn't I say I was fourteen? In a few months' time that would have been the truth. Oh well, it's too late now – if Fizz finds out I'll tell her it got lost in translation.

'What about you? How old?' He has to think about it.

'Six – teen.'

Sixteen, that's older than Fizz said! Thank God I said I was fifteen, he would never have been interested in a little thirteen-year-old. I feel much better now . . .

No I don't. You can cancel that feeling of warm relief. I have just had a ghastly, awful, embarrassing realization!

'Aaagh! I've forgotten to bring any money . . . No money!' I do a penniless orphan mime, pulling out imaginary pockets and gasping. I am so stupid, I can't believe it!

Oriol frowns at me. Either he doesn't understand or he thinks I'm a complete idiot. Of course he hasn't got any English money on him, only a few Spanish coins. We look round for a Bureau de Change, but that's far too exotic for Trewyss. It's Sunday, the banks are closed, we're starving hungry and we're stuck.

But Oriol turns out to be very resourceful sixteen-year-old. He looks around, at first I'm not sure what for, but it turns out that he's trying to find a suitable space. There's a raised platform on the quayside, next to the old lifeboat ramp where children dangle lines for crabs. The platform is surrounded by four benches, which are never free for more than a few seconds. As one family licks the grease off their fingers and throws away their chip wrappers, there is another identical set hovering, poised to grab the still-warm seat as soon as it's vacated. Altogether they make a captive audience of at least twelve people.

Oriol is standing in the middle of the platform. He takes a scarf from his old duffel bag and lays it on the ground. Now he's taken three juggling clubs out of his bag. He winks at me and tosses them gracefully into the air. He is brilliant! His sparkling brown eyes fix on the clubs as they fly from one hand to the other, effortlessly, beautifully. The families on the benches are entranced. Now other people are stopping, forming a circle round the platform. He passes the clubs behind his back, now under his leg – the crowd applauds.

Now he's going up to a little girl and asking to borrow her teddy. He's juggling with it *and* the three clubs – the crowd laugh and clap again, but they have no idea how difficult this is. Am I impressed or what?

'Excuse me, pleeez!' He waves the crowd back a few feet, and gestures for one of the families to get off their bench – normally this would cause a riot of protest, but they shuffle off willingly, thrilled to be somehow part of the act. He leaps onto the back of the bench, which is narrow and perilously close to the edge of the harbour, and carries on juggling, balancing on one foot. This guy's cool. And I mean really cool. The crowd goes mad! Oriol jumps off the bench and bows again. Then he steps forward and grabs me by the hand. Oh, no. Oh, no. What is this all about?

'You can do?' he whispers, waving his hands about. I know exactly what he's asking – oh how I wish I didn't understand. But if I'm going to have any chance with Oriol, I'm going to have to show him that I'm a circus performer, just like him. So, here goes!

He finds three silk balls in his duffel bag – phew, they're much easier than clubs – and throws them to me, one by one. 'Uno! Dos! Tres!'

I start to juggle. My palms are sweating and my heart is racing. Out of the corner of my eye I can see Oriol juggling with the clubs, dancing around our wooden stage, jumping, spinning, twisting. '*Ouai-ai-ai!*' he shouts to me, or something like that, and I nearly drop them.

Oriol puts down his clubs and back-flips across the platform – I don't know how he manages it, there's no room for a run-up! We hold hands and bow – as I look up I can see about forty people cheering and clapping. Then someone throws a fifty-pence piece onto the scarf. Then another. Most of the crowd leaves without giving us anything, but we still manage to accumulate £5.32.

'We're rich!'

'Feesh an' cheep!' cries Oriol. Not chips again, I think, but I run along with him to the Sea Shanty café. We are triumphant.

'You're wicked at juggling!' I gasp. 'Amazing!'

'You too – weecked!' he replies in that sexy accent. I'm sorry, but he's gorgeous. Utterly gorgeous.

We walk the length of the harbour, eating our chips and swigging cans of Coke. It's great not to have to think of something to talk about. Several people recognize us, and say hello. He's only been here a few hours and already he's a local celebrity. I'm not sure that busking is allowed in Trewyss – I've a feeling it's against the law. But so what? Nel Sharpe does that sort of thing, you know, she's very adventurous, not afraid of taking a few risks. Well, what do you expect from the daughter of Flying Fizz?

It's about five o'clock when we finally get back to the cottage. Rosa must have brought some food with her, because she and Fizz are in the kitchen chopping vegetables! I didn't know Fizz even *had* a chopping board! Correction – on closer inspection, Rosa is chopping vegetables and Fizz is watching her, yet another glass of wine in hand.

'Hi!' She waves. She obviously has no idea that we've been gone for three hours, so I'm not going to tell her anything about it.

'Have we got time for a swim?'

Fizz asks Rosa in Spanish and Rosa says, 'Si.'

Even I know that means yes. 'Want to go for a swim, Oriol? . . . Swim. In the sea.'

He turns his nose up and says something to Rosa. 'He says Engleesh water too cold!' she laughs.

Which is a bit of setback. Still, mustn't rush it. There's plenty of time. The tour starts tomorrow, and Oriol and I are going to be seeing rather a lot of each other. For once, reality has exceeded my fantasies. Dare I say it, but I think I'm in love!

CHAPTER FIVE

It's six o'clock in the morning and the kitchen is full of people who can scarcely manage a sentence without yawning. Nobody got to bed until 2 a.m., and we badly need reviving. But of course, there is no freshly-squeezed orange juice or egg on toast like we have at Dad's. Instead, our tired and grumpy hostess is making a pot of raspberry-leaf tea. This involves pouring boiling water over a lump of grey fluff that looks as if it's come straight out of a vacuum cleaner. You don't put milk in it, which is just as well, as we haven't got any. And at the moment we've nothing to drink it out of either. Rosa is currently making a tour of the cottage in search of mugs. I don't know why she's bothering. Take it from me, raspberry-leaf tea is disgusting.

You must be wondering why on earth we are up at this ridiculous hour. Well, today is the first day of the circus tour and we have to be in Somerset by 9 a.m. Fizz is not what you call a 'morning person', so she's being rather snappy with me. She's not being snappy with Rosa or any of the others, of course - either because they are guests or because she doesn't know how to be irritable in Spanish. Actually, I think I woke Fizz up by setting my alarm half an hour before anyone else. I had important things to do! I needed to shave my armpits (yes, again!), put on my sexiest hippie outfit and cover my eyelids in sparkly blue eye-shadow. The next part of the plan is to get to drive in the Los Diabolos van with Oriol.

Jordi has just handed round a packet of battered Spanish biscuits, which he probably found under the driving seat. They taste stale and the chocolate spread in the middle is a bit revolting at this time of the morning. But at least it's breakfast. I think I'm going to like Jordi. He doesn't say much, even in his own language – he's more of a 'doer'. I wouldn't be surprised if he turns out to be the only practical one among us, but in these early days it's hard to tell.

'Would you like Rosa to come with you, so you can chat in the car?' I mumble, hoping that I sound more spontaneous if I talk with a mouthful of crumbs.

'What, girls in the car and boys in the van?'

'Well . . . I don't suppose there's room for me in the back of Daisy.' This is ridiculous! Why do we always have to speak in code? Why can't I just say, 'Look, I really fancy Oriol and want to go in the van with him all the way to Somerset, OK?'

As it happens, I don't have to resort to the honest truth and the code works. I'm sharing the shaky, noisy van with Dídac, Jordi and Oriol as we bomb up the motorway towing the tiny caravan behind us. Mission accomplished, you'd think. Except I hadn't bargained for the fact that they would spend the entire journey speaking in Spanish! Actually, they're not speaking in Spanish, but Catalan. Fizz explained to me last night that people

42

who come from Barcelona speak their own language, which is like Spanish with a bit of ancient French thrown in. Luckily, Rosa and Oriol also speak Spanish – it's all very confusing! Anyway, they're chattering away and even singing in Catalan while I try not to fall asleep with sheer boredom. This I mustn't do on any account as I know I have a tendency to sleep with my mouth wide open. Hannah took a photo of me once on the way back from a school trip. It was not a pretty sight.

We arrive at the site just after 9.15. Brian, the chief organizer, waves us onto a muddy field. He's wearing an official Four Winds Festival sweatshirt and wellington boots. Obviously, that's not all he's wearing – I just didn't think his trousers were worth describing. Brian is here every year. Each summer he looks a little fatter and has less hair. In one hand he holds a megaphone and in the other is a clipboard with a pen attached to a length of string. These days he also carries a mobile phone and a portable radio. He hangs them diagonally across his chest so that they bounce off his stomach as he walks and hit him in the face whenever he bends over.

'Fizzy! Hello!' he booms through the megaphone as he marches towards Daisy. 'As soon as you've unloaded can you put your car in the campsite?'

Fizz winds down the window. 'But, Brian, I need somewhere safe to keep my fruit. I don't want anyone pinching my pineapples.'

Brian roars with laughter, as if Fizz has just made a dirty joke. 'And who have we got here?' Brian consults his clipboard.

I lean forward and shout out of the window: 'Los Diabolos!'

'Ah, yes, the caravan stunt.' He ticks us off with a flourish. 'Speak English?'

'I do!' I reply.

'You're right in the centre . . . Buenos días!' he adds in his best holiday Spanish.

There is a pause during which Brian expects a similar reply. But Jordi is not being rude, Brian's accent is so English that he just didn't realize that he was being greeted in his own language. (Although Spanish isn't his own language, is it? It's Catalan.) Poor Brian. His cheeks redden and he lets out a nervous laugh to fill the gap.

In some ways I like the before and after bits of these festivals more than the events themselves. You can watch the acts rehearsing without some dad plonking his kid on his shoulders right in front of you, and you can browse around the stalls without anyone trying to sell you anything. People smile at me and some of them even remember that I'm Fizz's daughter. It's as if we are all part of a huge family waiting for a load of party guests to arrive.

Fizz is busy setting up in the corner of the field. I ran over and offered to help but she just grunted and said hadn't I better go and apply some more lip-gloss in the ladies? What has got into her this morning? Los Diabolos are busy fiddling about with the caravan. Dídac and Oriol are checking ropes and hooks and Rosa is shaking out their costumes. A crane has just driven onto the field and the driver is having a hand-signing conversation with Jordi. Now Rosa is joining in – what on earth do they want with a crane?

I'm hanging around the van, feeling like a spare part. I have no job to do and not a clue what's going on, so I sling my bag over my shoulder and make my way towards the stalls – lots of earrings and bits of twisted metal threaded onto leather thongs. There are several stalls selling scented candles, wooden children's toys, velvet hats covered in shiny braid that never stay on your head, embroidered bags, Indian incense burners and hand-painted flowerpots. I have some spending money from Dad, who expects me to return with some present for him and Julie – it's all part of the pretence that I miss them. Julie collects owls, for some bizarre reason – soft toy owls, china owls, glass owls, owl mugs, owl engravings in slate, owl notepaper . . . the whole house is full of the stupid things. But it makes present-buying easy. I can usually find an owl something on my travels. As for Dad, well he's like most dads – impossible to buy for. Last year I bought him a painted stone paperweight for his desk, which he said would look better in the garden. The year before that I bought him a wind chime, which Julie insisted gave her a migraine so it went off to the charity shop. I suppose I'll have to buy three presents next summer. I hope my baby brother or sister isn't going to be so fussy, but with parents like Dad and Julie, it's not looking good.

I decide that it's too early in the holidays to start searching for owls. I'm feeling strangely drawn towards the Natural Healing tent. Every festival these days has a Natural Healing tent. This doesn't mean that there is no longer any need for the St John's Ambulance, which has just parked up next to the catering mobiles. If you cut your finger opening a can of Coke, or twist your ankle in a rabbit hole, then you still need to see the nice old gentleman in the navy jumper and his dull-looking teenage assistant who obviously has no social life. But if you feel out of sync with the universe, or your body is full of negative energies, then the Natural Healing tent is the place to go. You can lie on a blanket and some woman with spiky pink hair and patchwork dungarees will dangle crystals over your stomach. Or you can have your tarot cards read and be told that just because the Death card has appeared it doesn't mean you're about to die. No, no, no, not at all – the Death card simply means Change. The people in the Natural Healing tent are always positive. But then, who wants to pay a fiver to hear that they're about to have a fatal crash on the M5?

It's two o'clock in the afternoon now and the place is really crowded. It's a mixture of very straight-looking families having a 'nice day out' and New Age types with dreadlocks and dirty feet – people who look like my mother basically. If I try very hard, I can almost imagine Dad and Julie as part of the 'nice day out' camp. Dad would be complaining about the lack of decent toilet facilities and he wouldn't let me have a burger in case it gave me food poisoning. They'd find the place too crowded, too disorganized and too dirty, but they would love moaning about it in the car on the way home. On second thoughts, there's not a chance that they'd ever come to a place like this. Dad would be too terrified that Flying Fizz was one of the circus acts. No, they'd be off to the nearest National Trust property, to gawp at rich people's possessions and marvel at the enormous number of bedrooms. Tedious or what? . . . Give me a pair of Germans dressed up as penguins playing the saxophone any day!

And there they are! Wolfgang and Oskar – hobbling around the field, sweating like mad in the huge costumes which cover them from head to foot. You can see their faces in the beak – it looks as if a giant penguin has swallowed them whole and is still chewing on their heads. They talk in penguin language (so they say), which is nothing but high-pitched squeaks. They must have established some penguin words between them, because they always know when it's time to start playing. Their music is jazzy and lively and has a magical effect on grandparents and toddlers who start to dance, waving their arms in the air and swinging their hips from side to side.

Wolfgang and Oskar recognize me, and wave with their flippers as they come to the end of a song. I run over to say hello and they squeak a reply.

'Have you seen Los Diabolos?' Wolfgang whispers, temporarily coming out of character.

'Ve saw zem in Paris, zey ver vonderful,' adds Oskar. They both speak great English, but Oskar's accent makes me want to fall over with laughter.

A three-year-old starts to swing from Wolfgang's tail, nearly pulling his costume off his head. 'Eek! Eeeeek!' he squeaks in frantic penguin, but the child's mother is too busy wiping ice-cream off a baby in the pushchair.

'Careful, you don't want to hurt the penguin,' I say, gently prising away the kid's sticky fingers.

'Kids, eh? I cannot stand them,' Wolfgang whispers,

raising his eyes to the sky.

'I haven't seen Los Diabolos perform, but they're staying with us – with Fizz,' I explain.

'They are about to start, you must go!' Wolfgang cries, flapping a wing in the direction of their caravan.

I must be a complete idiot! Here I am, talking to overgrown penguins while Oriol – I mean, Los Diabolos, are about to perform! Got to run, got to get to the front of the crowd . . . Why won't all these people just get out of my way?

CHAPTER SIX

Phew . . . just made it . . .

I have pushed my way to the front of the crowd gathered by the Los Diabolos caravan. Fizz is there, dressed in a pair of glittery baggy trousers, a sort of home-made boob tube wrapped round her neck and tied across her back, and a gold turban on her head. She looks like a tatty genie who has lost her lamp.

'When are they going to start?' I ask. Fizz replies without diverting her gaze from the caravan. 'It's already started.'

'How come? Dídac isn't in costume. And where is Oriol? And the others?'

'Shhh, or you'll spoil the whole thing!' Fizz retorts impatiently. But what is there to spoil? All I can see is Dídac, sitting on a deckchair outside the caravan reading a newspaper! If someone doesn't start doing at least a handstand soon the crowd is going to wander off.

Then, from behind the Natural Healing tent comes the crane that I saw earlier in the morning. It's making its way towards the caravan, with Brian walking ahead, waving the crowds to either side. He has a very stern look on his face and his stomach is wobbling like a jelly at a child's birthday party. 'Out of the way, please!' he booms through the megaphone.

'That's Jordi, driving!' I gasp.

Fizz gives me a kick. Yes, a real kick, right on my shin. And she's wearing a pair of stupid Aladdin shoes with toes that curl upwards so it really hurts. 'Will you *shut up!*' she hisses and then swears at me!

Sometimes she is unbearable. I briefly consider stomping off in true teenage fashion, but actually, I want to see the act, so I swear back at her silently and stay put, looking as offended as possible. But even that is a pointless exercise because she's not looking at me.

'This is an arts festival, not a gypsy camp!' shouts Brian through his megaphone.

I can hear mutterings around me in the crowd. Dídac leaps up from his chair and starts waving his newspaper at Brian, while shouting in Spanish (or Catalan?). I want to ask Fizz what's happening, but I can't because I'm offended.

'We're going to have to remove you from the site!' booms Brian.

The crane moves towards the caravan while Dídac gesticulates and shouts and even begs on his knees to be left alone. I'm not sure whether the crowd realizes that this is all part of the act.

Jordi, who is wearing a pair of blue overalls and a cap pulled down over his eyes, is throwing metal ropes over the roof of the caravan and hooking them onto the side. Dídac raises his fist in anger and lets out a torrent of abuse. Jordi doesn't reply, not wishing to spoil the illusion that he is in fact a local crane-driver who just happens to look identical to the Spanish gypsy. He walks back to the crane cab and switches on the engine. Dídac appeals to the crowd for help and some of them boo Brian in support. Brian turns round and hisses at them as if he's in some Christmas pantomime.

But this is not enough for the seemingly distraught Dídac, who has rushed into the crowd and has grabbed a hostage − a woman dressed in a headscarf and long raincoat. I realize that Rosa has been standing a few feet away from me all the time. Dídac flings open the caravan door and shoves Rosa inside as it starts to rise into the air. A young boy dressed equally warmly in jeans and a heavy waterproof coat runs after the woman and cries out, 'Stop!'

'Oh yes, er, stop!' shouts Brian, as if he has just remembered his lines. 'You can't do that!' He has a huge grin on his face. Acting is definitely not Brian's strength, but he is having the time of his life. Screams and bangs are coming from inside the caravan, and I hear a mum turn to her children and say, 'I'm not sure this is suitable for you,' but they beg to be allowed to stay. The caravan is several feet from the ground now and the boy − of course it is Oriol − has grabbed hold of a hook and is dangling in mid-air.

'I hope he's all right,' I murmur without thinking.

At last Fizz turns and looks at me. 'Don't worry,' she whispers very quietly. 'They're real experts, even your Oriol.' Why did she say that? He is not *my* Oriol − not yet anyway . . .

But I can't think about all that now. Oriol is climbing up the side of the caravan and onto the roof. It's swaying in the air several metres above the ground now and the audience are gasping and wondering whether they should applaud or fetch the man from the St John's Ambulance. Oriol bangs on the roof with his fists. The door suddenly flies open and Rosa almost falls out, but Dídac drags her back in and slams it shut.

The caravan is getting higher and higher. There are more bangs and shouts from inside and coloured smoke starts to emerge from a side window. Then two trapezes are dropped through and Rosa climbs out, wearing a sparkly red leotard and fishnet tights, followed by a bare-chested Dídac in black skin-tight trousers. The crowd sighs with relief and applauds madly.

Rosa and Dídac swing on the rope as they unhook parts of the caravan wall, which seem to fold away miraculously into the sides. I can't really describe the mechanics of it — it's a bit like writing up a physics experiment, and science is not my best subject. Anyway, we are now looking at the inside of a perfect gypsy caravan, with a tiny dresser covered in plates and a table bearing a vase of flowers and china teacups. The crowd laughs, I suppose, because nothing has been knocked off or broken despite the fact that the caravan has been tossed around like a ship in a storm.

And what has happened to *my* Oriol? you are no doubt wondering . . .

Well, he's still standing on the roof, and has just unzipped his waterproof coat. Now he is ripping off his jeans from the waist in one extravagant and (it has to be said) very sexy gesture. Just as I'm wondering how this trick works, I become horribly aware of a number of other teenage girls in the crowd who are whistling and cheering as if Oriol is doing a striptease. In fact, that's precisely what he is doing. He has thrown off his T-shirt and is bare-chested – and I mean bare-chested: not a hair in sight (unlike Dídac, who has hair up to his neck and all over his back). He is now wiggling his hips in a pair of extremely tight-fitting black trousers which, I have to say, don't really suit him. His legs are too thin for them, although it doesn't bother me, being a stick insect myself. And with a bit of luck it will put off the competition! But this is not the time for an analysis of Oriol's body. I should be watching the show. Oriol opens a window in the roof of the caravan and jumps inside. Rosa and Dídac do the most amazing acrobatics on the trapeze while Oriol starts juggling with a stack of plates that have been sitting on the dresser.

'Awesome!' I shout, applauding hard as they eventually slither down the ropes and somersault onto the grass. The three of them take a bow and gesture towards Jordi, who whips off his feeble disguise and waves.

Fizz claps enthusiastically, then grabs my arm. 'I'm on next. Come on!'

'But, Fizz, can't I just stay for a minute to say well done to Ori—?'

But she cuts me off. 'No, Nel! I need you!'

As she drags me through the crowd I turn back, trying to catch Oriol's eye. But he doesn't spot me. Now he's going to think that I'm not interested, and those girls who are giggling their way towards the front are about to pounce.

Ten minutes later my extraordinary mother is balancing a melon on her nose and juggling with bananas. I wonder about her sometimes. Is she a bit mad? OK, so she has purple hair and never wears socks, but sometimes I think that maybe there's more to it. I never know what to expect from her. One minute she's giving me little presents and telling me how much she loves me, and the next she's ignoring me or making foul comments. And I don't know what I've done in between. Why has she been so horrible to me today? Is it because I dared to take an interest in a gorgeous boy of about my own age? I don't know – maybe she was just nervous about her show.

She needn't have been. She's great. Fizz has a real way with audiences. She jokes with them and gets them involved in the act. To be honest, she's nothing like as skilful as Rosa, who is leaner and stronger and probably braver too. But Flying Fizz makes people laugh, although she doesn't do any flying any more. She gave up trapeze work a long time ago, but the name just stuck.

Perhaps it was just nerves: as soon as the crowds finish applauding and disperse, she rushes up and gives me an enormous hug. 'Was I OK?'

'You were great! So funny!'

'I'm so glad I didn't drop anything – that was the first time I've performed that routine in public, you know,' she gasps, as breathless and excited as a child. 'Come on, let's find the others . . . I'm sorry I dragged you away; I just needed you, Nel – I needed you to be there.'

Now she's holding my hand instead of gripping it and we're threading our way through the thinning crowds. The festival is almost over and people are starting to make their way home. Ahead of us we can see Rosa and Oriol. Fizz runs up and embraces them. Oriol winks at me and I literally go weak at the knees. The teenage girls are nowhere in sight. Suddenly everything is right with the world.

Right now I'm sitting on a small wooden stool, having a henna tattoo applied to my shoulder – a few tickling strokes of brown ink that spell 'Love' in Arabic, or so they tell me. Oriol, my potential boyfriend (note the word 'potential' there, please), is standing next to me, trying to decide between a dragon and a snake for his forearm. I'm happy again. I can take Fizz's sarcastic remarks or the occasional kick with an Aladdin slipper. If you want the ups, you've got to accept the downs along the way. (Eleanor Sharratt is not at all sure that this is true, but she is fading far into the distance, and right now her opinions don't count.)

CHAPTER SEVEN

It's Monday morning and I'm sitting on a bench at the quayside of Trewyss. It's about time I wrote Dad a postcard. He never rings me at the cottage in case Fizz picks up the phone, and Fizz suddenly gets worried about her phone bill if I ask to phone him. So we have to resort to the old-fashioned postal service. Really grown-up behaviour, eh? It annoys me so much! I have made a promise to myself that if I ever get divorced I'm going to remain good friends with my ex-partner. But of course there is the small matter of finding a husband first!

Anyway, this parental stupidity is the reason why I'm staring at this jolly snap of fishing boats in the harbour. What on earth am I going to write? How about: 'Dear Dad, Sorry not to have been in touch sooner. I'm having a great time here in Cornwall' . . . Mmm . . . should I be having a *great* time? Does he want me to have a great time? Or would he rather hear that I'm having a lousy time and that I wish I were with him? Maybe I should just cut the adjectives out altogether. And if I write in big letters I won't have room to say much.

Dear Dad,

Sorry not to have written sooner. We've just got back from a week of touring. We've been to Somerset, Devon and Land's End. It rained twice. Hope you and Julie are well. Will write again soon. Love, Eleanor.

There, that's done. Now for my postcard to Hannah! I've bought one of those fold-out letter cards, with about six different photos on the front and heaps of room on the back so that I can give her the full low-down on what's been going on.

Hello Hannah!

Having a fantastic time with Fizz. Guess what – this gorgeous Spanish hunk is staying with us – he's an acrobat and he's sixteen!! We've spent loads of time together and he's teaching me to juggle with four clubs and do back flips. You can keep Craig Basford, he's just a creep compared to Oriol! He's got dark wavy hair, long eyelashes, brown eyes and he's taller than me. Phew! We've been to loads of festivals this week and I've been riding in the van with Oriol every day. We're sitting closer and closer to each other on the back seat, so I think he likes me. But it's not easy to get off with someone when parents are around the whole time!

Oriol's mum, Rosa, is just about the sexiest mother I've ever met!! She is really slim and beautiful. She and Fizz are great friends and they never stop giggling, but they speak in Spanish so I haven't a clue what they're laughing about. Hope it's not about me and Oriol! He is soooo fit! His dad is nice too – his name is Dídac. He's really hairy and he plays the guitar and he's always mucking about and making jokes. He sings Catalan songs (bit like Spanish) really loudly in the street, which is embarrassing! Oriol's parents seem to get on ever so well – I haven't noticed a single row, which is pretty amazing. Jordi is Dídac's twin brother. He's great too, much quieter than Dídac. He's not an acrobat, he does all the driving and fixes things. They do this incredible stunt with a caravan, really high up in the air. I wish you could see it. I wish you could meet Oriol, I'm sure you'd like him, but you're not allowed to fancy him because he's mine! At least I want him to be. We get on ever so well, but it's not easy to get to know someone when they don't understand most of what you say. I'll have to use body language instead!!!!

Oh bother, I've run out of room.

I squeeze in a 'Love E', as if she didn't know who it was from, underline the word 'gorgeous' and 'fit' and put the postcards in the post-box before Fizz asks to read them. Not that I need to worry too much, I think she's accepted that Oriol and I are going to be more than just good friends. Fizz is cool. She sees that I'm growing up and doesn't have a fit at the thought of me having boyfriends. Her act is going down really well, even though Los Diabolos keep stealing the show, so generally she's in a very good mood. Why else would she be in the supermarket with Rosa, buying food?

Oriol, Dídac and Jordi – 'the boys' as Rosa calls them – have gone on a speedboat trip with a group of tourists. I was going to join them, but Fizz pulled me to one side and pointed out that I get horribly seasick. Did I really want Oriol to see me heaving up my lunch over the side? So when I saw that the rest of the party didn't contain any female rivals I chose to play it cool for once and stay here. It's a relief, to be honest, not to be in Oriol's presence all the time. If I flutter my eyelashes much more they'll fall off!

I'm pretty certain he likes me. After all, we have a lot in common and I don't suppose he meets many other girls from circus families. I've never done so much juggling practice in my life. A couple of days ago he stood behind me, really close, reached forward and took my hands in his.

'Like thees,' he murmured, showing me how to throw in a steadier rhythm. Of course I dropped every single club! But so would any girl if a gorgeous boy was standing so close that she could feel his breath on her neck? I mustn't get too excited here. I've got to think, to plan. The problem is how to take the friendship to the next stage. We've four more weeks to go. Four weeks of seeing each other every single day . . . something's *got to happen.*

The 'boys' have just got off the speedboat and are walking down the jetty towards me. Oriol is laughing and talking with his hands, his T-shirt and jeans are soaking. He looks like a model in one of those black and white adverts for French perfume or a poster in a trendy café – well, from a distance anyway.

'Rosa?' questions Dídac. I point towards the Co-op. He and Jordi go to help carry the shopping, leaving Oriol alone with me. This is a rare moment, and somehow I've got to make the most of it. If only Hannah were here, she could tell Oriol that I like him and ask him if he wants to go out with me. That's what usually happens at home. But that's pretty pathetic, when you think about it – having to get a friend to do all the negotiating. No, I've got to land this catch by myself!

'You're wet,' I say. He frowns. 'Water – wet. You are wet.' I gesture at his clothes and he shrugs as if to say it doesn't matter. Another even longer pause.

Oriol starts to walk along the harbour front, looking in the shop windows, and I follow him because I'm not sure what else to do and I can't bear to let him go off by himself. I stop when he stops and we stare silently at the named mugs and toothbrush holders. I'd like to buy him a little present to give him a clue to how much I like him, but the chances of finding anything with 'Oriol' painted on it are absolutely nil.

'Remember when we did that busking?' I say as we arrive at the jetty. He looks at me blankly: he obviously doesn't know what busking means. I mime doing the juggling and he nods, but I don't feel that he's really understood. He doesn't seem in a very good mood today. I wonder if he's missing his friends in Barcelona. What if he already has a girlfriend waiting for him back there! Nobody's mentioned anybody, but that doesn't mean she doesn't exist. This is unbearable! My mind is working overtime, trying to interpret every look, every gesture. All I can think is: Is this the way a boy behaves when he fancies you? Or are we just friends? Or are we not even friends? How can I know if we can't talk to each other? Oh, why didn't I choose Spanish instead of German as my second foreign language? And can somebody please come and rescue us from this awkward situation before I throw myself off the harbour wall?

'Oriol! Nel!' Rosa is shouting to us.

I breathe an audible sigh of relief and scamper over to the grown-ups, who are waiting by the public toilets, their arms full of plastic carrier bags.

'Rosa is cooking paella tonight,' announces Fizz. 'It's a traditional Spanish dish.'

'Great!' I reply. 'But do we have six plates?'

It's a warm evening and we're eating in the garden. Fizz has stuck candles in the grass and laid her bedspread over the rickety garden table. Jordi is sitting on an upturned bucket and Dídac and Rosa have squeezed together on the wall. The rest of us are sitting in Fizz's tatty old deckchairs, which are so low that you have to stand up to reach the table.

'This is delicious!' I enthuse.

Rosa pulls a face. 'No, it's not good. It is not the real paella,' she says. 'I cannot buy the . . . how you say? . . . azafran . . . I do not know the word in Engleesh . . . it make the rice yellow, yes?'

'Saffron,' explains Fizz irritably, having heard all this before. 'And Nel's right, the meal is absolutely fine. In fact, it's great!'

'It is not great! There is no feesh!' (She means fish.)

Oh dear, I wish I'd never said anything. Unfortunately, there was a bit of a scene in Trewyss earlier on because Fizz wouldn't let Rosa buy any prawns or mussels from the fish market. Apparently paella without prawns and mussels isn't paella at all – it's just vegetables and rice.

Fizz insisted that she wasn't having 'murdered animals cooked in her kitchen', which was a rather extreme way of describing a pound of prawns, and made Rosa explode in a torrent of Spanish. Then Dídac joined in the argument and it all became very loud and embarrassing. There was a lot of arm-waving and shouting and at one point Dídac dangled his shopping bags over the harbour wall, threatening to toss them into the sea.

Oriol and I decided to keep well out of the way. We sat on the car-park bollards and shared a bar of clotted cream fudge in an awkward silence, trying to pretend that these theatricals were nothing to do with us. Jordi managed to stay out of the fish row too, but I think he's regretting it now. He's obviously not very impressed with the paella. He keeps searching forlornly through the rice with his fork, as if looking for a prawn that's miraculously found its way into the meal. A funny thought suddenly strikes me: in the meat- and fish-eating department, Los Diabolos would get on far better with Dad! I imagine them meeting up for a steak and complaining about 'bloody vegetarians'. Of course, it'll never happen, but my imagination plays with the idea for a while.

'Let's play a game on the beach,' I say, quite out of the blue. I'm quite taken aback by this outburst. Eleanor would never make such a spontaneous suggestion, but Nel – now she's a girl of the moment, always full of fun ideas. More importantly, I've realized that the party desperately needs cheering up.

Fizz finds a warped old bat and some bamboo canes in the shed and announces that we'll play cricket. Dear old Jordi finds a tennis ball in the van. He is always finding things we need in that old crate – I'm starting to think it must be magic, an Aladdin's cave full of useful treasure!

The 'boys' have no idea how to play cricket. I suppose they don't play it much in Spain. Fizz explains the rules and divides us into two teams. It was my idea to play, but she's put herself in charge. Fizz is on one side with Jordi and Oriol, and I'm put with Dídac and Rosa. I wish she'd put Oriol and me on the same side, but maybe it's better not to be too obvious. Dídac goes in to bat first and Fizz appoints herself bowler. She starts off trying to bowl overarm in true cricket style, but the balls only travel about two metres, which sends the adults into hysterics of laughter. Oriol and I don't find this quite so amusing, but then, we haven't just drunk three bottles of wine.

Once we've reduced the gap between the stumps and Fizz has resorted to bowling underarm the game gets going. Dídac has very strong arms and fantastic hand–eye co-ordination, so he gives the ball an enormous thwack and it flies off towards the sea. Jordi chases after it and picks it up just before a wave is about to sweep it away.

Dídac is running between the stumps, which is completely unnecessary as surely the sea counts as the boundary. I shout, 'Six!' and everyone stares at me.

'Fizz, did you explain about fours and sixes?' I ask her.

'No, I forgot!' she shouts back, laughing. 'I just said hit it and run!'

Dídac's next shot goes way up into the air and is an easy catch for Jordi. 'Howzat!' I cry, but nobody has a clue what I'm talking about. Now it's Rosa's turn.

She is so beautiful, I can't take my eyes off her. It's quite windy down here on the beach and her jet-black hair is blowing across her face like a scarf. She is wearing a tight white T-shirt and black jeans, which she has rolled up to the knees. Her toenails are painted scarlet. There's not an ounce of fat on her body, and yet she's not skinny. Her skin is tight and deeply tanned, but if you look closely at her face you can see a bridge of freckles across her nose. Rosa looks like a fiery flamenco dancer, and if she hadn't chosen to work in the circus I think that's what she would have been.

Rosa stands ready for Fizz's ball. As it flies through the air, she steps back and twists her body round . . . then whack! The ball zooms across the sand like a bolt of lightning. I watch it bounce into the rock pools and shout a triumphant 'Four!' but nobody is listening. They are clustered around Rosa, who has fallen to the sand and is clutching her side.

'What's the matter?'

'I'm not sure,' replies Fizz.

Rosa is crying, biting her bright red lips with agony. Dídac bends down and takes her in his arms. He is talking to her in urgent Catalan, but Rosa can hardly catch enough breath to reply.

'How could she have hurt herself hitting a tennis ball?' I persist.

'Shhh.'

'Perhaps it's appendicitis?'

'Nel, please be quiet!'

I turn to Oriol, but he doesn't seem to know what's going on either. Jordi and Dídac are helping Rosa to her feet. She can walk, but is obviously in terrible pain. Dídac carries her up to the cottage and lowers her gently onto the sofa. With the aid of her Spanish dictionary Fizz discovers that Rosa thinks she has done something to a rib. Apparently, Rosa had a bad fall from a trapeze last year and was in hospital for several weeks. Even now, her ribs can 'pop out' and crack very easily. I can't begin to imagine what 'popping out' means, but Fizz tells me it's something to do with the connection to the spine. I don't want to know the gory details.

'Fizz – we can go to hospital?' says Rosa, weakly.

'Yes . . . but it will take ages for an ambulance to get all the way out here. It would be quicker to go straight away in my car.'

So Rosa is laid on some cushions in the back of Daisy, and Fizz, accompanied by an anxious and very tearful Dídac, drives them away into the night. I know Fizz has drunk far too much wine to be driving, especially down those unlit country lanes, but I don't say anything. Hopefully, she'll be driving slowly so as not to disturb Rosa.

Oriol and Jordi decide they are not going to bed until

the others return. It's dark now and I can't stop yawning. Nobody talks much, but I've a pretty good idea what we are all thinking: How can Los Diabolos perform without Rosa? I suppose they'll have to cancel the shows and go back to Barcelona. It's so unfair, just as Oriol and I were . . . Oh, I mustn't even let myself think about that . . . But I know they won't want to cancel – they need the money – Fizz has told me how thrilled they were when she managed to find them the bookings. Oh why, oh why did I have to suggest we played a beach game? I've wrecked the tour and put Oriol's mother in hospital. There's no way he is going to be interested in me now!

CHAPTER EIGHT

I've just woken from a fantastic night's sleep – which is really odd considering how depressed and guilty I felt when I climbed into bed. The sun must have woken me up – I was so tired that I stupidly forgot to draw my curtains last night. It must be ever so early. I raise myself onto my elbows and look out of the window. The triangle of ocean that sits between the cornfields is sparkling like a turquoise party dress. If I'd come here for a seaside holiday, I'd be bounding out of bed and packing my beach bag. I peer at the clock. Half past five . . . aaargh!

I don't know what time Rosa, Fizz and Dídac got back from the hospital. It must have been late because I went to bed at 1 a.m. A horrible thought hits me – what if they're not back yet? What if the injury was so serious that they kept Rosa in? Half of me wants to hide under the blankets, and the other half wants to leap out of bed and find Fizz. I'm desperate for the loo, so I've got to get up anyway – I might as well discover the Awful Truth right now.

But Fizz is not in her room. I can't tell whether she's slept in her bed because she never makes it. I can hear voices in the sitting room below. I run halfway down the stairs to see everyone else already up and dressed, and in the middle of some urgent discussion. At half past five in the morning? What is going on?

Rosa is lying with her legs up on the sofa. She's not covered in plaster or bandages, but she looks very tired. Jordi is sitting in the same chair as he was last night and the others are sitting on the floor. Nobody's noticed me, so I sit on the stairs and try to understand the conversation from their tones and gestures. The only word I can make out now and again is 'Nel'. They're probably saying, 'If it wasn't for Nel and her stupid games, we wouldn't be in this mess.'

Everyone is wearing the same clothes as yesterday – of course: they're not up early, they haven't even been to sleep yet. It seems as if I was the only cold, uncaring member of the group who tripped off to bed. I'm about to creep back to my room and try the hiding-under-the-blanket option when Fizz looks up and sees me.

'Ah, Nel, you're up. Come and join us.'

I slowly descend the stairs. Will bunny pyjamas pass for daywear? Not a chance. I feel like a criminal, caught in the act of slumber.

'Rosa's old injury has flared up, I'm afraid. It means she's going to be out of action for a few weeks.'

'Oh, no . . . I'm sorry.'

'Well, these things happen. It's a good job it wasn't in the middle of a performance – she could have had another fall. The real problem is, how are Los Diabolos going to continue with their act?'

'We need three persons or it's not working,' says Rosa.

'Dídac has to take somebody hostage so that Oriol can

68

go after them.' Fizz pauses. I look around the room and realize that everyone is looking at me.

'We want you,' says Rosa.

'Me? What about you, Fizz? You could do it easily!'

'Yes, I know I could, but we think it should be you. You look more like a member of the general public, for a start. If my show's on first, people will recognize me.'

'Not if you're wearing a hat!'

'Even then, it might be tricky. What if I have to do my show straight after? I wouldn't have time to change into my costume. Anyway, sometimes we're scheduled to perform at the same time. No, it makes far more sense for you to do it.'

'But I've never been on a trapeze!'

'You don't have to do any aerial work, or even juggling. We've worked it all out. Dídac will take you into the caravan and hook you up on a harness. Then, when the sides come down, all you have to do is stand in the corner, looking terrified.'

'Well, at least the last bit will be easy,' I joke. 'Do you really think I can do this?'

'Of course you can!' says Fizz, turning to say something in Spanish.

Everyone immediately nods and cries, '*Si! Si!*' Oriol says several sentences, smiling and looking at me all the time with those divine brown eyes.

'Oriol tell me you are very good,' says Rosa. 'He says you are best Engleesh acrobat girl he knows. He wants you very much, he says you are his special friend and you must join our family!'

Wow! Did he really say that? I can feel myself blushing. But I mustn't take the words too literally: Rosa probably hasn't made a terribly accurate translation of what Oriol actually said.

'See? We all have absolute faith in you,' Fizz adds enthusiastically. 'I promise, darling, you'll be perfectly safe.'

'We must go now, so you have time to rehearsal it,' says Rosa.

'We're going to get the crane to arrive early,' explains Fizz, 'so we need to be there as soon as the site opens. So hurry up, darling, we've got to get going.'

Oh well, it looks like I've agreed to be part of the show!

Dídac immediately picks me up and carries me giggling towards the door. Oriol tells him to put me down (I think that's what he said) and then puts his arms around me and gives me this really tight hug. What a moment for our first embrace – I haven't had my shower, I've got no make-up on and I'm still wearing my pyjamas!

'Thank you, Nel. I am sad for my mother, but I am very happy you with me.'

I can hardly believe this is happening – I am very happy he's with me too! Is this boy the most adorable hunk on earth, or what?

So, here I am, several hours later, at the Westward Festival. I'm standing in the crowd with my pretend boyfriend (if only that were true!), waiting to see Los Diabolos perform. Oriol has his arm round my shoulders, which would normally be more than enough to account for my weak-at-the-knees feeling, but in fact it's pure terror. My mouth has gone completely dry and the jumper I'm wearing to hide my harness is making me feel so hot that I think I'm going to faint. I know Nel Sharpe likes an exciting life, but this is ridiculous.

I should point out that I haven't actually been up in the caravan yet. We got stuck in a traffic jam on the way here, and by the time we arrived there were members of the public on the site so we couldn't 'rehearsal it'. Nor is there any sweet, blobby Brian at this particular festival – just some unfriendly, over-tanned blonde woman in a white jogging suit, who has reluctantly agreed to pretend to evict Los Diabolos from the site. All in all, the omens are not good. Perhaps I should pop over to the tarot stall to see what the next hour has in store for me. No doubt the Fool card will turn up. I wish Fizz was here with me, but she's gone to perform on the other side of the field, having first pressed her lucky topaz into my sweaty hand. She never performs without it, so that probably means I'm going to be fine and she's going to have an accident . . . Stop it, Nel: don't even think such things.

'OK?' whispers Oriol. I nod and smile weakly. Of course I'm not OK!

The crane has arrived. Dídac has put down his newspaper and is looking questioningly at Jordi. I vow to myself that I will never, ever suggest another game of cricket for as long as I live. I wouldn't be surprised if Los Diabolos sat up all night trying to devise this as a punishment. I realize that I'm not a circus girl at all, I'm just a silly thirteen-year-old who can juggle a bit and wobble about on a unicycle. Oh my God, Dídac is running towards me ... Too late to back out now!

We're up ... the caravan is lurching about horribly. Why didn't I take a travel tablet? The only thing I could possibly throw up in is that vase on the table. But I happen to know that in a few minutes time Oriol will be juggling with it, so I'd better not. I keep telling myself that I am 'perfectly safe' surely my own mother wouldn't let me put my life at risk ... Would she? My brain is not working in sympathy with any other part of my body. I'm meant to be screaming for help, but no sounds will come out. Dídac is making high-pitched noises to compensate, whilst banging on the walls and changing into his costume at the same time. If I weren't terrified out of my senses, I'd be fascinated to see how the stunt is done from the inside.

Oriol must have climbed on because I can hear him scrambling up the side and onto the roof. Dídac is sorting out the trapeze and getting ready to set off the coloured smoke device. He's having to do everything by himself and he's really sweating. I watch in silent amazement as he opens what looks like a teapot and smothers his hands in chalk. He hooks and unhooks the ropes, checking and re-checking. There is no safety net under the caravan, just a patch of worn grass. It suddenly occurs to me that this is probably how Rosa had her accident last year and I catch the taste of my lunch in my throat. Whatever happens, I must not be sick.

But the worst is yet to come: Dídac has climbed out of the window, leaving me quaking in the corner. Oriol stamps his foot on the roof to give the signal, the front of the caravan swings away and I'm clinging onto the sides for dear life. I daren't look down at the crowds, but I can hear them applauding, even cheering. Now Dídac is on the trapeze and Oriol is throwing plates a few inches in front of my nose. It's probably not as spectacular as when Rosa is performing with him, but I couldn't tell you for sure as I've got my eyes screwed shut. If this is what I have to do to be Oriol's girlfriend, then we might as well forget the whole romance now.

Of course I don't really mean that.

'Fantasteek! Fantasteek!' I can hear Rosa shouting from the crowd. At last we're back on solid ground. I'm holding Dídac's hand and bowing like a real circus performer. I just wish bowing didn't involve so much bending forward. I need to find the nearest mobile toilet before I throw up all over my feet.

'Ouai! Chulu!' cries Oriol, spinning me round in a celebratory dance (actually that should be spelt 'Guai' and 'Xulu', but then you'd have no idea how to pronounce it). 'Nel no es anglesa, es catalana!' (meaning I'm not English, I'm Catalan, which is probably the highest compliment he could give me). Dídac does three backflips and then breaks into one of his extraordinary folk songs, while the more practical Jordi runs to the van and fetches a bottle of wine. He doesn't say anything, but he looks pleased. No doubt he's relieved that we got through it safely. Fizz and Rosa join us after a few minutes and everyone toasts my success. What a day! I can hardly believe it's all over, still less that they expect me to do it all over again at six o'clock – and twice a day for the next four weeks!

'You are good actor,' says Rosa. 'You looked very

73

scared up there, I believe you!'

'That wasn't acting. I was terrified!' I gulp. 'But thanks.'

'I know what we should do in between shows,' Fizz announces. 'Let's get you a nose-stud! I know you've been wanting one for ages.'

Yes, please!

The tiny blue stone above my nostril feels like a New Age medal for bravery. It hurt a little when it first went in, and now it's sore. I keep putting my hand up to feel the stud even though Fizz has warned me that it'll turn septic if I fiddle with it too much. Mmm . . . I think I can do without a nose that oozes pus – not ideal when it comes to snogging.

I've a feeling a snog might be on the cards – I shouldn't call it a snog: it sounds really immature. Let's call it a proper kiss. All the signs are there:

1. After the six o'clock show, which went really well (and for some weird reason didn't make me feel sick at all), we stopped off in a pub on the way home and Oriol deliberately sat next to me.

2. He ordered exactly the same food as me and he didn't take his eyes off me all evening.

3. And this is the surest sign of all: we are now sitting in the back of the van together, really, really close, making our way back to the cottage down the dark Cornish lanes. Oriol reaches out and takes hold of my hand. Now he's stroking my fingers! His touch is really soft and gentle, and it's sending shivers up my arm and all over my body. My heart is pounding almost as much as when the

caravan first rose into the air. He has put his head really close to mine; I know he wants to kiss me, I can feel it, but nothing can happen with Dídac and Jordi sitting in the front seats! We'll be back at the cottage soon. It's too dark to suggest a walk on the beach. If this proper kiss is going to happen, there will have to be A Plan. If only I had a telepathic communication line to Hannah, she could tell me what to do next!

Familiar sights come into view – the post office/restaurant and the clotted cream tea rooms, the local primary school at the top of the hill. We rattle down into the bay and turn left along the dirt track. The sea is just a black mass, but we can hear it roaring in the darkness. I step out of the van and pretend that I need to stretch my legs, to breathe in the night air. Has Oriol got any ideas of his own, I wonder, or am I going to be left out here by myself like a total idiot?

Oriol and Dídac help Rosa out of Daisy and take her round the back. Jordi locks the van, picks up his cigarettes and wanders into the house. Then Dídac comes out again and stands next to me, inhaling the salty smell of the sea. This is getting stupid. Doesn't he realize that Oriol and I want to be alone? I've been waiting for this since the moment I first saw him, asleep in the back of the van.

A few ridiculous minutes pass by. At last Dídac goes back indoors, but Oriol doesn't re-appear. Fizz sticks her head out of the window and asks me if I want a drink. Of course I don't want a drink – I want a kiss! It's no good, I've obviously misread the signs yet again. I heave a huge sigh and walk as slowly as is humanly possible round towards the back door.

Oriol is standing there, finishing a cigarette. He smiles at me and takes my hand. He is looking particularly gorgeous in the moonlight. 'Nel, here,' he whispers. Oh dear, this is sounding really soppy, isn't it?

The proper kiss is about to happen, and it's as much as I can do to stop myself leaping on him like an excited labrador! I've got to calm down or I'm going to make a mess of it. Mustn't bang noses, mustn't clang my brace on his teeth. What should I do with my arms – put them round his neck or his waist?

Mmmm . . . This might be my first kiss, but it obviously isn't Oriol's! He seems to know exactly how it's done and I bet he hasn't been practising with a pillow. His lips are really soft, and he tastes of tobacco mixed with strawberries (which we had for pudding at the pub). It's a combination I'm going to remember for the rest of my life. It's a rather long kiss and I'm starting to wish I'd taken a deep breath first! But I'm not going to be the one to end it: I want it to go on for ever.

Of course it can't go on for ever, or I'd suffocate to death. Oriol pulls away and gives me a slow, sexy smile. My knees are actually trembling – honestly! He strokes my cheek and whispers something in Catalan that I wish I could understand, because I've a feeling it's something really sweet and affectionate. But I'm completely dumbfounded. I can't think of a thing to say (except the obvious 'I love you' and I've read enough magazine articles to know that that is a really bad idea). So, I just smile back like a fool, my brace no doubt twinkling like a row of tiny stars. But I don't care about it any more – having a mouth full of metal doesn't seem to have put him off one bit.

After several more amazing kisses (I remembered to breathe through my nose – much easier) we walk into the cottage – to a round of applause from the grown-ups! It turns out that they have been watching us from Fizz's bedroom window. I start to act all offended, then realize that's the way Eleanor would react, not Nel. Oriol's not in the least embarrassed and pecks me on the cheek just to prove it. I catch a glimpse of myself in the mirror over the fireplace and see that I'm still grinning from ear to ear. My nose is feeling sore, I've an earring missing and my mascara's smudged, but that's the price you pay when you have several proper kisses! I'm so sorry, dear Rosa, that you cracked your ribs, but thank you . . . thank you.

'Oh, look, we've got a message,' says Fizz, glancing at the answerphone.

'Let's leave it till the morning,' I reply dreamily.

'No, we'd better not. It might be about tomorrow's gig.' Fizz rewinds the tape and everyone stops talking to listen.

'Er . . . hello . . . this is a message for Eleanor,' it starts.

'Who is Eleanor?' says Rosa, but Fizz motions her to be quiet.

As I hear my father's voice my blood runs cold through my body. 'Er . . . can Eleanor please give me a ring. Straight away . . . It's urgent.'

'Do you want to ring him now?' asks Fizz.

'I don't know. He sounds upset . . .'

'It's up to you, darling.' Fizz picks up her glass of wine

and perches on the end of the sofa. The Spanish chatter starts again. Oriol-looks at me worriedly, not understanding why I've gone as white as a sheet.

Dad wouldn't phone here unless he absolutely had to. Something awful must have happened. But what?

CHAPTER NINE

Funny how the weather can change to fit your mood. Yesterday's sunshine has vanished, the sky is a wash of grey and it's pouring with rain. Large blobs of water are making their way slowly down the outside of the window and forming a dirty stream along the bottom edge. I draw a heart in the cloud of condensation and then rub it out. What's the use? I'll probably never see him again. Not that I should even be thinking about Oriol at this moment, there are more important things to worry about than my love-life.

I'm on the train, making my way back to Dad, Julie and my new baby brother, who was born yesterday afternoon. So why am I not celebrating? Why didn't I zoom into the nearest Mothercare and buy a blue sleep-suit and a shiny card saying 'Congratulations – it's a Boy'? Because he (no name has been mentioned yet) has arrived thirteen weeks early and it's touch and go whether he will even survive.

When I rang Dad late last night he answered the phone in a thin treble – as if he'd been expecting the call to be from the hospital, telling him it was all over. He sounded in such a panic that I hardly recognized his voice. 'Get Felicity to put you on the first train in the morning. I'll meet you at the station. As fast as you can, Eleanor. I can't tell how much I need you to be here. The whole family should be together. It's important, you understand. I want you to see him . . . just in case.' Just in case he dies, I suppose. This is awful. I don't know if I'm going to a celebration or a funeral.

What do I feel about all this? I mean, *really* feel . . . It's very hard to work it out. Having a baby brother should give me a feeling of excitement, shouldn't it? And discovering that he might die should make me feel desperately sad. But I don't feel either – just grey and dull, like the weather. I am trying hard to feel what I ought to be feeling, but it just won't come. It reminds me of the time a girl in the sixth form choked on her own vomit and died at a party. Everyone else in the school was wandering around looking tragic and tearful, but I couldn't even remember what she looked like – although I was assured that she'd once told me off for jumping the dinner queue. The more I tried to feel as if I had suffered a great loss, the more I found myself smiling. I couldn't stop it – it was really embarrassing. It wasn't that I didn't care about her, it was just that I couldn't keep the sadness going hour after hour, when I didn't really feel it. I need to get in touch with my feelings – and fast. If I turn up at the hospital with a grin on my face Dad will hate me for the rest of his life.

I keep going back over our brief conversation last night. Dad said something about the baby having 'immature lungs'. What does that mean exactly? Is it something that will get better by itself? Or will he need an operation, even a transplant? We might have to go on television and appeal for someone to have a car accident and donate their organs. And if he survives, is he going to have 'special needs'? Will we move to a bungalow to accommodate his wheelchair? Will we start parking in the disabled spaces outside the supermarket? Is my whole life about to change for ever or is this just a horrible phase we've got to get through and then get over?

A wave of guilt sweeps over me as I realize that this baby isn't just a bump in Julie's stomach, he's an actual human being. I do hope he's going to be all right. Maybe now Dad won't make so much fuss all the time and concentrate on being grateful that his children are alive. Sometimes you need an experience like this to make you realize what's really important in life. Oh dear, this is getting very deep, isn't it? I need to change the subject.

Just before we left the cottage this morning Oriol gave me a farewell present – beautiful silk juggling balls, emerald green, midnight blue, and scarlet, covered in tiny sequins and swirls of embroidery – the ones he lent me when we busked in Trewyss, that first afternoon we met. They're sitting in my lap at the moment like a clutch of eggs for three exotic birds. I lift each one to my nose and sniff, hoping to catch a smell of the circus, or of Spain, or even of Oriol himself. He must be keen on me, or he wouldn't have given me his favourite juggling balls. Hang on, I've just made that up. How do I know they are his 'favourite' juggling balls? Maybe they've been festering at the bottom of his kit bag for the past three years and he was about to throw them away. Why can't I be content with the fact that he gave me a present? He wouldn't have given me anything if he had wanted to put me off, would he?

'Eleanor!' It takes three shouts of my name before I realize he's talking to me. Dad is already at my side and flings his arms around me, holding me so tightly that the metal anarchy sign on my leather necklace digs into my chest. As I ease myself away, I see that his face is pale and unshaven – he looks ten years older than when I last saw him, as if he hasn't slept for a week.

'What – is – that?' he says slowly, pointing a quivering finger at my nostril. Of course this is not a genuine question so I don't bother to reply with the genuine answer. 'Take it out, this instant!' he cries, snatching my bags from me. This is easier said than done, as we are now on a crowded escalator.

We haven't made it to the car park yet and already he's told me to undo those stupid plaits, take off that filthy rag (I presume he's referring to my new skirt) and have a bath before he can so much as consider taking me to see Alexander. Which is Dad's sweet way of saying, 'Welcome home, and by the way we've chosen a name for your new baby brother.' So much for Dad discovering that there are more important things in life.

I feel as if I'm playing Misfits – that game where you split pictures of people into parts and swap them around. My head and body are Nel's, with Eleanor's face wedged uncomfortably in the middle. Dad is driving bad-temperedly round the one-way system while I attempt to remove the stud with the aid of the wing mirror. The tiny hole starts to bleed.

82

'Sorry. I'll take it out as soon as we get home.'

'How could you do this to me?' he mutters. 'After everything we've been through these past few days.'

This is confusing. Did I attempt to put a nose stud in Dad's left nostril? No. Did I plait my hair, get a henna tattoo painted on my shoulder, paint my toenails and wear a tie-dye skirt in a deliberate attempt to upset him? Of course not. I just forgot to put on my Eleanor costume this morning – the neatly ironed jeans and pink cotton shirt that I usually save for the return journey. It didn't seem important. Obviously I was wrong. 'I'm sorry,' I mutter lamely.

'Well, it's a bit late now. In the circumstances, Eleanor, I thought you would have had more sense.'

Ah, yes, but you see it is Eleanor who has the sense, and she hasn't been around for the last few weeks. But there's no point explaining this to Dad, because he wouldn't listen, let alone understand.

'How's the baby – I mean, Alexander?' I mumble through my brace.

'Well, it's still touch and go. He can't breathe by himself and he's not holding his temperature. There may be other problems too. But they won't know till we get the results of the tests.'

'Oh dear . . . And how's Julie?'

'Distraught, as you can imagine. And she had to have a Caesarean. Look at your feet – they're caked in dirt. I'll have to take you home first. The special care unit has to be sterile, you understand. I have to wash my hands in special germicide for three minutes before I can even open the incubator. They won't let you in, looking like – like some . . . some gypsy!'

I'm back in Eleanor's bedroom now, with its matching duvet and curtains, its fitted wardrobes and windowsill lined with soft toys. I turn to the mirror for a last glimpse of Nel before I reverse the transformation spell. She looks more grown-up than Eleanor, tall enough to pass for at least fifteen, maybe older. I like her hair, I love her sparkly make-up, I adore the twinkling nose stud. Her multi-coloured skirt curves round her tiny waist like an escaped rainbow, her long thin legs are slightly tanned, her long toes painted alternately pink and silver. I smile at her and give her a small wave. 'Goodbye, Nel,' I whisper to the reflection. 'See you again, sometime . . .'

When I come down the stairs an hour later, Dad breathes a sigh of relief and says, 'That's more like it. I've got my little girl back.' He gives me another stifling hug. 'I'm sorry I shouted at you, it's just that I'm under a lot of strain at the moment. Nothing's turned out the way I imagined. I was assuming you'd be here when the baby was born. I wanted the four of us to be together, right from the start.' His eyes start to mist up. 'At times like this, it makes me realize how much we all need each other. I'm so glad you're here, Eleanor.'

'Me too . . .'

'I've really missed you. It's not the same when you're away. I keep wondering where you are or what you're doing. The house feels empty without you. It's too quiet. Would you believe it, I even miss the sound of your dreadful music!'

'I've missed you too,' I mumble. But I haven't really, have I? I feel really guilty – but more for not missing him than for lying.

'Still, that's enough of feeling sorry for ourselves. Come on, let's go and see your baby brother.'

I thought Julie and Alexander would be staying in our local maternity hospital, but they've been transferred to a special unit some forty miles away, where they have better equipment for looking after very premature babies.

'How long will he have to be in hospital?' I ask as we pull out of the driveway and head for the main road. The best help I can give is to sound positive, to assume that Alexander is going to live.

'A long time, I'm afraid,' Dad replies. 'They usually keep premature babies in until the time they should have been born.'

'So that means another thirteen weeks?'

'I'm afraid so. We're looking at late November, maybe even December.'

That's such a long time . . . I don't want to be sitting in our clean, tidy car, with tedious classical music softly playing on the radio. I want to be in the Los Diabolos van, swinging down the country lanes with Jordi forgetting he's meant to be driving on the left side of the road. I want to hear Dídac singing his heart out in his Catalan folk songs. I want to feel Oriol's fingers reaching out for my hand on the back seat. I want to smell his hair, to touch the back of his neck. I want him to kiss me again. I want . . . I want . . .

'Here we are,' says Dad. 'And lucky for us there's a parking space.' My imaginative wanderings screech to a halt as Dad reverses the car with utmost precision – parallel to the two white parking lines and exactly in the centre of the space. I realize I'm feeling nervous about seeing the baby – what's he going to look like?

The hospital sprawls out before us like a miniature town – high-rise buildings, shiny industrial units and neat flats connected by small roads. The maternity department is housed in a tall tower that looks more like an office block. Dad tells me that the SCBU (Special Care Baby Unit) is on the sixth floor. We ring the bell and wait for a nurse to show us in.

It's like entering a spaceship – everywhere is white and machines are bleeping all around us. On the walls are hundreds of photos of smiling babies and happy toddlers on tricycles – the success stories, I suppose, put there to keep the parents' morale up. Julie is sitting in the corner, so close to an incubator that she looks as if she's guarding it. She gives me a feeble wave and puts her finger to her lips.

And here he is.

'I had no ideas that babies could be so tiny!' I whisper to Dad. We peer into the incubator as if it's the window of a sweet shop, containing all that's magical and delicious in the world.

'Just look at his little fingers,' he replies. 'Do you know, he only weighs as much as a packet of sugar.'

So this is Alexander James Sharratt. My baby brother – half-brother. My father and my stepmother's son. After Dad and Fizz, this tiny stranger is my closest relation in the whole world . . . I can't stop staring at him, loading every little detail into my memory. I want to be able to remember this picture of him for ever, so that when he's older, I can tell him exactly what he looked like when he was two days old. I'll tell him he was like a little skinned rabbit, his face as pink and squashy as a raspberry, his arms and legs no thicker than my fingers . . . I'll say he was wearing a thick woolly bobble hat over his ears that made him look as if he were about to go outside for a game of snowballs.

But Alexander won't be playing in the snow for a long time, poor thing. He has a tube going into his nose, which is taped onto his cheek, and more tubes leading from his arm, which is strapped to a splint. There are round pads on his chest, attached to leads, which are plugged into his monitoring equipment. The machines bleep constantly and make green zig-zagging patterns across the screen. He is fast asleep, his tiny fists clenched against his cheeks, concentrating with all his might on the enormous task of staying alive.

At last my eyes are blinking with tears. I'm not sure if it's sadness or happiness, but it doesn't matter. It's a feeling, an emotion. 'Hello, Alexander,' I whisper. 'It's your sister Eleanor here.'

CHAPTER TEN

Five days have passed and guess what — we're still sitting round the incubator staring at Alexander. As usual, he's fast asleep. The highlight of our day is when he wakes up and opens his eyes — huge, baby-blue eyes, rather like mine. We smile and say 'Aaaaaaah' in adoring unison. Then he closes them again! Babies have no idea how easy it is to entertain people. If they did, perhaps they'd do it more often. But no, Alexander wants to sleep . . . and sleep . . . and sleep . . . I lean my hand wearily on the lid of the incubator and one of the monitors starts bleeping loudly.

'Nurse! Nurse!' cries Julie anxiously. 'The alarm's gone off again! Nurse!' A large woman in a navy uniform and pink belt arrives and calmly resets the equipment. 'What's wrong with him?' Julie asks, nervously twisting the belt of her fluffy pink dressing-gown.

'Nothing,' replies the sister. 'I expect somebody banged the incubator. The machine's over-sensitive, that's all.'

Hmmm . . . It's not the only over-sensitive thing round here. As the nurse walks away Julie gives me one of those 'if looks could kill' stares.

'I didn't bang it,' I protest. 'I just touched it!'

'You've got to be more careful, Eleanor. This is a hospital! You're not at the circus now.'

Yes, well, I'd gathered that. I haven't spent the last few days somersaulting over the furniture or swinging off the curtains, although it would have been a lot more fun if I had. All I did was touch the lid with my finger! But I don't reply, I just roll my eyes to the ceiling and heave a long, irritated sigh.

I'm not saying this because she's just told me off, but honestly, Julie looks awful. Her hair is limp and greasy, she's not wearing the usual ton of make-up, and she's got shadowy bags of tiredness under her eyes. She refuses to leave Alexander's side, even though there's nothing she can do. He's only allowed out of the incubator for brief cuddles, and Julie can't breastfeed him. I suppose I should be more understanding. It can't be easy for her having stitches and all the worry of Alexander being so poorly, but she's stretching our patience to the limit . . . Well, *my* patience. I'm not sure about Dad's.

'She didn't mean to do it,' he explains gently, stroking Julie's hand, but she is not convinced.

'I can't have her thumping around, letting alarms off, Colin. My nerves won't stand it.'

Oh, so now I'm thumping around as well, am I? Fine! . . . In that case I'll just 'thump' over to the other side of the room and 'thump' myself down on a chair by the window. I'll stare at the cars in the car park instead. Hopefully, I can manage that without setting any alarms off.

'Don't take offence, Eleanor,' Dad sighs after me.

Too late, Dad. I've taken it – a great big lump of the stuff, in fact.

So what has happened over the past five days? I can tell you in one word: *nothing*. Actually, I suppose that's not entirely true. The results of most of the tests have come through and everything is looking very positive. The consultant has assured us that Alexander's lungs will grow to their proper size and there doesn't appear to be anything wrong with his heart or his brain. So panic over, you might think, but it hasn't stopped Julie weeping her way through a box of mansize tissues. Dad has spent a fortune on petrol zooming up and down the motorway, and I've read every woman's magazine published over the last five years (well, that's how it feels, anyway). Every day is so similar to the one before that I'm losing all sense of reality. I'm not living at all, I'm just watching replays of a video entitled *Eleanor's Hospital Visit*, showing daily between the hours of 10 a.m. and 8 p.m.

Half an hour passes. I refuse to look at either of them, but I can hear Julie sniffing and blowing her nose and moaning about how hospitals make her constipated, and how she'll never have a flat stomach again. 'If I ever have another Caesarean,' she tells Dad, 'I'm going to have a general anaesthetic. It was horrible! Like someone washing up inside your tummy.' Do we really have to know every detail? Dad makes sympathetic noises and says he understands how she feels. 'No, you don't,' she sobs. 'You're a man! You have no idea what I'm going through!'

Dad foolishly decides to change the subject. 'I remember the day I brought Eleanor home from the hospital,' he says fondly.

Uh-oh, *Wrong thing to say, Dad*! I'm cringing with embarrassment, fixing my eyes firmly on a licence plate that reads MOO. I may not know anything about what it's like to be a new mother, but one thing is certain: Julie will not wish to be reminded of the fact that Dad has been through all this before with another woman. At least he said 'I' instead of 'we', conveniently erasing Fizz from the story. But that's only because he can't bear to remember that she played any part in the event, not out of sensitivity to his suffering young wife. Just as I suspected, Julie has zapped into Quiet Mode, which is meant to signal to Dad that she's mortally offended.

Unfortunately, Dad hasn't spotted this; he is too busy digging an enormous hole for himself. Now he's telling Julie all about how he used to be up for hours, pacing the bedroom with me on his shoulder, singing 'Rock-a-bye, Baby'; how sometimes he would have to put me in the car and drive round the block until I fell asleep . . .

Yes, it's all very interesting, Dad, but please stop now! He still hasn't realized that Julie is annoyed with him, so she's had to resort to Plan B. This normally involves storming out in a huff. But as Julie can barely walk because of her stitches, this is not having the desired dramatic effect. You cannot hobble out in a huff, it just doesn't work.

'Going to the toilet?' enquires Dad innocently. 'Would you like some help?'

'Go to hell!' shouts Julie.

Dad is mystified. 'What's wrong now?' he sighs as she disappears through the swing doors.

'She doesn't like you talking about when I was a baby. She wants to pretend I don't exist.'

'Don't say such things, Eleanor. Julie's just over-wrought, that's all. She's been through a lot.'

'But it's true, Dad . . . I complicate things, just by being here. Julie's too young to be my mother, and I wouldn't be allowed in here if I were her sister. So who am I? I can only be your daughter, so it's obvious that you've been married before. Julie's a first time parent, but you aren't. She doesn't want to be reminded of the fact. She wants to play Happy Families and I spoil the pretty picture of Mummy, Daddy and their new baby boy. It's that simple.'

'You've got it wrong, Eleanor. It's not like that at all. Julie thinks a lot of you. She wanted you here the moment Alexander was born.'

'No she didn't. *You* did.'

'We both did. You're just as much part of this family as anyone else. We belong to each other. All four of us.' He gives me a tight squeeze and kisses my forehead.

I don't make any reply. Eleanor has said far more in the last minute than she usually comes out with in a month. Oh, Alexander, you've no idea how complicated life can be . . .

After a few minutes of embarrassing silence Julie returns, her face puffy with crying, and reclaims Dad's grovelling attention. Phew! . . . Somebody puts a lunch tray in front of her: white fish swimming in a thin yellow sauce, a splodge of floury potato and an orange jelly for dessert. Julie announces that she can't eat when she's upset and refuses even to lift her fork. So Dad eats it for her instead. No amount of emotional trauma seems to affect *his* appetite.

The hours drift by. All the programmes on the television in the lounge seem to be set in hospitals, and I feel as if I'm slowly going mad. A doctor arrives and takes some blood from Alexander's foot. Dad dares to read the paper and is told off by Julie for not noticing that she nearly fainted when she saw the needle. I go to the cafeteria and buy a can of Coke . . . Julie writes down a list of things she needs from home: clean underwear, some cotton wool pads, lip balm . . . A nice lady comes past with afternoon tea . . . Julie has her blood pressure checked and the nurse suggests that she go back to the ward for a rest, but she refuses to leave. I'm allowed to buy a bar of chocolate, having first promised that it will not 'spoil my tea'. I don't see how it is possible to 'spoil' the grey meat pasty, overcooked baked beans and soggy chips that we have an hour later in the hospital cafeteria. I've never tasted anything so disgusting. Dad apologizes for not being able to cook for me properly. How long are we going to have to go through this? I wonder.

We wander back to the SCBU to spend another hour Alexander-gazing. Julie tells us that while we were out he opened his eyes again. Isn't that just typical? The most exciting event of the day and we missed it!

I know this sounds mean and unkind. I know there is nothing that Alexander can do which would make the visits more entertaining, and we should be grateful that we haven't had any emergencies to liven up the day. But it doesn't stop me from feeling utterly and completely *bored stiff*. There, I've said it – it's out. You may think I'm a rather selfish teenager, but please, don't hate me for it. Try to understand what it's like, sitting there, hour after hour, day after day, with nothing to do. It's even worse knowing that my Wicked Stepmother doesn't even want me there. (Actually, that's rather a glamorous description of Julie, which she doesn't deserve.) I don't know why Dad is making me tag along every day. I know he thinks it's important that 'the family sticks together through the crisis', but I've got to *do something*, or I shall die of boredom. Is it possible to die of boredom? I must ask a doctor.

'Do you think I could see Hannah tomorrow instead of coming here?' I suggest to Dad cautiously as we drive home.

'Don't you want to be with Alexander?'

'Of course, but he's out of danger now, isn't he? And I haven't seen Hannah for weeks. She *is* my best friend.'

'All right, then. Give her a ring tonight. But you'll have to stay there all day. Julie won't like it if I have to leave early to collect you.'

No, Dad, but she'll be thrilled to bits to have me out of the way. Of course I didn't say that. The first rule of being a teenager is: If you're getting what you want, don't wreck it!

Oh, Hannah, please be around tomorrow! Please don't have to visit your auntie in Lichfield, or go shopping for new school uniform with your mum. I've so much I need to say and there's nobody else in the world I can say it to. Please be free to see me. Please, please, please!

CHAPTER ELEVEN

It's hard to describe just how great it feels to be sitting on Hannah's bed, having a huge girlie gossip! She even makes me feel good about being Eleanor Sharratt again. Hannah only knows me as Eleanor – she's never met my Nel self and somehow I don't think it would work. How awful it would be if the two of us weren't friends – it doesn't bear imagining. We've been best mates since primary school and we've only ever fallen out twice in all those years. Hannah and Eleanor share the same sense of humour, and have idential tastes in clothes and music – *and* boys, unfortunately. But there's no way she's getting her hands on Oriol. I've told her every bit of the story leading up to the 'first proper kiss' and we've spent most of the day in hysterics of laughter.

It makes such a change from being in the hospital, where we have to sit around looking anxious and concerned because Julie thinks being happy is 'inappropriate'. The fact is, Alexander is making good progress, considering some of his vital organs have yet to finish growing, and we should be celebrating. But you daren't say that to Julie because she says it's 'tempting fate' – what on earth does that phrase mean? It's as if she's in some sort of competition with the other mothers to see whose baby is the sickest. Sorry, I shouldn't have said that, but really, she's being impossible.

'Don't keep on about Julie,' says Hannah. 'Tell me more about Oriol. When are you going to see him again?'

'I don't know . . . ' I sigh with all the heaviness of someone deeply in love. Because I *am* deeply in love, I really am. 'They're only in England until the beginning of September, and then they go back to Barcelona. I might never see him again . . . '

'But you've got to!' screams Hannah. 'You can't let a catch like that get away.'

'He's not a fish!' I laugh, but she's right. I've got to see him again. If we don't stay in touch, he might forget me – or find another girlfriend. I just couldn't bear it!

'I know! You could text-message him!'

'He doesn't have a mobile. And nor do I.'

Hannah admits this is a slight drawback. 'What about e-mail? Does he have e-mail at home?'

'I don't think so. Los Diabolos are artists, not office workers.'

'Well, some artists must have computers.'

'They couldn't afford one – you should see their van, it's falling apart.'

'Then how on earth are you going to keep in touch?'

'Write to him, of course!' I grin.

'Letters! Of course!' gasps Hannah, as if they were the latest development in communication technology. 'And make sure you get him to send you a photo! I can't believe you haven't got one to show me. Unless he isn't as gorgeous as you say. Maybe he's really short and fat and covered in spots!'

'What, like your Jason?' I spar back. Hannah has just got back from Cyprus, where she had a brief romance with a fourteen-year-old with short hair, fat cheeks and an obsession with Newcastle United.

'That is so not true!' retorts Hannah. I snatch her photo of their two grinning faces in the hotel swimming pool and wave it at her triumphantly. 'Those aren't spots,' she insists. 'They're freckles!'

'No way! They're spots!'

And so the hours go by, one minute teasing each other, the next discussing how it feels to be in love, and how different it is from what you read in magazines. Privately, I don't think Hannah's experience in Cyprus can really compare with my relationship with Oriol – I mean, she only met Jason on the last day of her holiday – but I let her believe we are in an equal state of passionate despair. After all, what are best friends for?

'Oh, I don't think I can bear to go back to the hospital tomorrow,' I sigh as we recover from our twenty-third giggling fit.

'I can't believe you'll have to keep going there every day! I mean, I love babies and all that, but he could be there for months!'

'He will be! I don't know what's going to happen. Julie thinks she can get some kind of hospital flat. She wants us to stay with her, of course. But the hospital's forty miles away! How will I get to school in the morning? I'll have to get up at five o'clock. And Dad will never make it in time for work.'

'I think you should come and stay with me,' says Hannah. 'Not for ever. Just until the baby's well enough to come home.'

'Oh, Hannah, that would be awesome! We'd have so much fun! Do you think your mum and dad would mind?'

'I shouldn't think so,' said Hannah. 'Of course, the other person you could go and stay with is Fizz . . .'

It's as if she's switched a light on in my brain. 'Hannah, you're a genius! I mean, I'd love to stay with you, you know that, but if I went back to Cornwall I'd see Oriol again.'

'Exactly!' beams Hannah. Fortunately, she is not easily offended. 'You'd have to go to school there, of course. I bet they have schools on the beach in Cornwall – that would be so cool! You could go swimming every day! I'd miss you like mad, but maybe I could come and visit . . .' Hannah continues making all sorts of arrangements for how we will keep in touch, musing whether her mother would let her come down to Cornwall by herself at half-term, deciding what clothes she might take, whether she needs a new bikini (she's obviously never been to Cornwall in October) – ridiculous details I stopped listening to ages ago.

My mind is whizzing round. This is the perfect solution! Dad could move into the hospital flat with Julie and I could be with Fizz for a whole term! 'Hannah, you are the most fantastic person in the whole world!' I cry, excluding Oriol of course, but that goes without saying. 'It would solve so many of Dad's problems, he'd be a complete idiot not to say yes!'

'True, but parents often *are* complete idiots,' replies Hannah thoughtfully. 'You'll have to put it the right way. Don't sound too keen on the idea. And don't forget to say how much you're going to hate being away from Alexander.'

'That's a good point . . . I mean, I will miss him and all that, but . . .'

'And don't say anything negative about Julie.'

'Of course I won't.'

'And you'd better ring Fizz first, just to make sure she doesn't mind.'

'Yes, yes I will!'

Well, so far so good, I followed Hannah's instructions to the letter, phoning Fizz while Dad was in the shower. 'Of course you can come, if you really think you'll like it,' she replied airily. 'I think there's a school in Northquay you could probably go to. Get your father to sort it out.'

Dad wasn't so much of a pushover. He bit his lip and made considering noises, finally saying that he'd 'sleep on it'. That's all very well for him, but of course it meant I hardly slept at all, wondering what his decision was going to be. He didn't mention it once over breakfast, and I decided not to say anything in case I sounded too keen on the idea and made him suspicious. But the agony of waiting!

We're in the car now, off to the hospital again. I can't bear it any longer. I've *got* to say something, but it's got to sound casual, as if I don't mind either way. OK, let's go for it . . .

'So, have you had a chance to think about my idea of going to Cornwall?'

Dad keeps his eyes firmly on the road ahead. I'm glad he's not looking at me, I'm sure I'm trembling all over.

'Well . . . it would certainly ease the strain here – if you're sure you wouldn't mind, Eleanor . . .'

If I wouldn't mind? Keep calm, girl, keep calm! 'I'd miss Alexander, of course, but you could phone me with progress reports.' Dad grimaces. He obviously doesn't like the idea of phoning the cottage in case Fizz answers. Time for some quick thinking. 'Perhaps I could get a mobile phone, then we could keep in touch as often as we liked.'

'Yes, that would be a good idea. But what about going to a different school? I wouldn't like to disrupt your education . . .'

'It's only Year Nine, Dad. It will be ever so hard on you if I stay, looking after me every day with Alexander still in hospital. And poor Julie having to stay in the flat all by herself. She's been through so much lately, I think she needs you to be with her.' That last bit was rather sick-making, wasn't it? Perhaps I'm over-doing it.

Luckily, Dad doesn't seem to think so. 'Yes, that's true . . . I'm quite worried about her. She's been very depressed. Well, Eleanor, it's a very kind thought. We'll discuss it with Julie. Let's see what she says.'

Oh dear, it's so hard not to smile and jump in the air with delight. What a good job I'm in the car and have my seat belt to restrain me! If the decision rests with Julie, I'm home and dry. She'll probably secretly crack open a bottle of champagne when Dad tells her. I feel a bit mean, pretending I'm making a huge sacrifice for the sake of the family, when all I'm doing is thinking about myself. But what the hell? I'm going to buy Hannah a huge thank-you present for this. I'm going back to Cornwall! To be with Fizz! And I'm going to be with my Oriol again! Yesssssss!

Whoosh! The past two days have flown by . . . Here's a very quick summary: as I predicted, Julie could barely hide her delight when Dad put the suggestion to her. Perhaps she's turning into my Wicked Stepmother after all. Dad rang up the Cornish education what'sit and found me a place in a new school. It's several miles away, but apparently there's a bus that tours all the villages. He's bought me a mobile phone – the cheapest one available so it's like having a tank in your pocket, but never mind. He's also opened a savings account for me with a cash card and a secret number, so I can get hold of money when I need it – he's put in £300 for the term! Incredible!

I've sorted out what I'm going to take – just about everything I possess actually. I'm only taking a few Eleanor clothes, but my entire collection of CDs, my photo albums, even my passport. I want to be prepared for any eventuality. Fizz sometimes gets bookings abroad, and I'd have to go with her. Best not to mention that possibility to Dad: he'd hate me having time off school. Oh, I am sooooo excited!

So, Saturday is the big day. I shall give Alexander my full sisterly attention at the hospital tomorrow, and be really sweet to Julie even if she makes one of her bitchy comments to me. And on Friday night I'll shave my legs and armpits and pluck my eyebrows (why are beauty treatments all about removing hair?) and put on a face-mask and try to get some sleep, if I can. I do hope Alexander will forgive me for leaving him like this. He's only a baby, I'm sure he has no idea that I even exist. He can't possibly miss me, can he? And it does make life easier for Dad if I go to Cornwall . . . Sorry, I'm wittering on now. I'd better go downstairs and watch some boring television with Dad: *act normal*, that's the thing to do, Eleanor, *act normal*. You're so close, you mustn't blow it now . . .

CHAPTER TWELVE

So here we are again, back at the same service station on the motorway. It's five to three, and I'm in my lookout position in the restaurant, scanning the car park for Fizz's arrival, while Dad hides behind the sports pages of the Saturday paper.

'She'd better not be late,' he murmurs, glancing at his watch. Actually, I forgot to tell Fizz that Dad needed to get back to the hospital. But maybe that was just as well – if she knew she might well turn up late deliberately. The minutes tick by. Dad heaves several irritable sighs and takes his temper out on the newspaper, which is refusing to fold neatly. 'Perhaps you'd better take the train in future,' he said. 'It worked out all right the other week, didn't it?'

'Yes, it was easy . . . '

'It's not that I mind taking you by car . . . '

'I know. But if I went on the train, there wouldn't be the slightest chance of you and Fizz seeing each other.'

'It's not that I don't want to see her,' mutters Dad.

'Yes it is! You hate her.'

'She hates *me*,' he replies defensively. Note that he didn't deny it.

'Well I think you're both pathetic.'

'Eleanor! That's not fair. You don't know how difficult it is.'

'Of course I do! I'm stuck in the middle, remember?'

'I know . . . I'm sorry . . . But I don't want you to have to witness any unpleasantness. Believe me, it's better this way, for your sake.'

Oh yeah, it's all for my sake. Honestly, Dad, how stupid do you think I am? 'She's here!' I shout.

Dad leaps to his feet and gives me a hurried hug. 'Good luck in your new school. I'll ring you on your mobile . . . And don't forget to do your homework . . . and make sure you eat properly and—'

'Yes, Dad. You'd better go now.'

He glances anxiously around and dashes out of the restaurant, speeding down the stairs and into the shop like a terrified rabbit. Not that he minds meeting Fizz, ooh, no . . .

Actually, she hasn't arrived at all. I just suddenly felt compelled to make him go. I shouldn't have done it, but all this hiding from each other really gets on my nerves. I hope he walks out of the shop in five minutes' time and bumps into her in the car park. It'll serve them both right. Anyway, I feel like being on my own for a while. I've some adjusting to do. I take out my magazine and read an article entitled 'Summer Romances – Do They Ever Last?' The answer is definitely 'no', according to a group of girls interviewed in Ibiza. 'You'll be lucky if your love affair lasts as long as your tan,' it says. I hope Oriol and I are the exception! There's only one week of the holidays left, seven days until he goes back to Spain.

Is that long enough to get a proper relationship going? Well, I suppose I'm about to find out!

'Nel!'

It's half an hour later and I look up to see not only Fizz, but Oriol too! I'm not sure whom to greet first – although of course I know whom I most want to embrace! Fizz rushes forward and squeezes me tightly. Then Oriol gives me one of those Spanish kisses – one on the left cheek, one on the right. I'd have swapped them both for one on the lips!

'Oriol insisted on coming with me!' cries Fizz. 'He couldn't wait to see you.'

'I couldn't wait to see him,' I enthuse. It seems funny greeting him wearing my Eleanor disguise – not that he appears to have noticed anything different about me. Perhaps there's not as much difference between my two selves as I thought. Interesting eh? But I haven't time to delve into that too deeply . . .

'I very happy . . . you here,' says Oriol, picking up one of my suitcases. He mutters something in Catalan. By the look on his face I think he's just complained that it's heavy.

'Sorry, I just brought everything I could think of.'

'Are you staying for good?' laughs Fizz.

Well, it's a tempting thought.

Oriol and I sit together in the back of Daisy as Fizz drives us back to the cottage. She looks like our chauffeur, not that I've ever seen a chauffeur with purple hair and huge dangly earrings. Oriol keeps hold of my hand the entire way, which is not as pleasant as it sounds. It's a hot day and my palms are sweating. Fizz and Oriol speak to each other in Spanish and then she gives me the gist of what they've said. I want to say a few things to Oriol, but I'm too embarrassed. How can you say, 'I've really missed you,' or 'I've thought about you constantly,' when your mother has to translate it into another language first? I have *got* to learn some Spanish, or Catalan even! I wonder if Fizz would teach me? In the meantime, we're going to have to make do with Oriol's English. Or maybe we won't need any words at all. I'm sure he can tell from the dreamy look in my eyes that I'm madly in love with him. And I have to say, his eyes are looking pretty dreamy too! This is exactly the sort of reunion I'd hoped for – better than my hopes, in fact. I must text message Hannah and tell her all about it.

We arrive at the cottage by late afternoon. Rosa, Dídac and Jordi are relaxing in the garden. Rosa is lying down with her head on Dídac's lap and he's playing affectionately with her hair. For some strange reason Jordi is trying to mend the door of the shed. Fizz won't have asked him to do it – I suppose he just likes to have something to do. They seem really pleased to see me, and greet me like I'm a long-lost friend. I have to say I feel closer to them than I ever do to Julie, whose hugs are always stiff and cold.

'At last! You are back!' says Rosa. 'You can perform with us again!'

'Yes, I can't wait!' I reply. In my absence, Fizz has been running between the two shows, putting on wigs and different costumes in the hope that the audience won't realize who she is. It seems to have worked out all right, but Fizz is exhausted and is only too glad to be handing the job back to me.

'Shall we go for a swim?' I ask Oriol.

'You'd be better off going this evening, when everyone's gone home,' interrupts Fizz, before Oriol can reply. 'It's like Piccadilly Circus down there.'

I walk to the edge of the cliff and survey the scene below. Fizz is right, the beach is ever so crowded today – dotted with families who have staked out their sandy territory with windbreaks and blankets. The sea is heaving with people: grandmas in old-fashioned swimsuits trying not to get their hair wet, kids knocking into each other with their surfboards, toddlers jumping over the dribbles of waves and shrieking as if they were foamy monsters. And beyond the hordes of holidaymakers are the local surfboys who have their own wetsuits and can stand on their full-size boards. They bob about in the deep water waiting for the few decent rides, while the tourists throw themselves onto their boards at the slightest opportunity and trundle triumphantly to the shore.

If I were blindfolded I'd still know exactly where I was. The familiar mixture of ice cream and salt wafts upward on the sea breeze. Distant cries of laughter mingle with the roaring ocean – the sound of hundreds of holidaymakers generally having fun. But somewhere below there will also be a crying baby who has just fallen over in the sand. A dad will be shouting at his children and a brother and sister will be arguing over whose turn it is to dig with the best spade. It's been like this for as long as I can remember. Of course, Fizz hates the beach in summer, but I love it, because it's exactly these sounds, sights and smells that make Cornwall feel like home.

'I can't wait,' I declare. 'I'm hot and I want to get wet.'

'OK. We swim!' replies Oriol. Luckily, he doesn't ask the others to join us, and we walk down to the beach hand in hand, looking to the rest of the world like a proper boy and girlfriend. I'm feeling pretty good in my new bikini – so glad I did all that de-hairing last night!

'It's better if we run in!' I shout to Oriol. 'Come on!'

The sea is as freezing as I knew it would be, and he jumps back in shock. 'No! No! No!' he shouts, running away.

'You'll get used to it. You will be OK!' I promise, dragging him back into the water. Oriol shakes his head and protests. The poor boy, he's used to the warm Mediterranean. 'Jump over the waves – you'll soon get warm!'

Suddenly Oriol lifts me high into the air, spins me round and then chucks me headfirst into the water! I stand up, spluttering, with a mouth full of salt and a length of seaweed caught round my ear. It can't be a very attractive sight, and if someone like Craig Basford had done that I'd be storming back up the beach in a temper. But instead I smile sweetly and flutter those long eyelashes of mine. Perhaps it's an old Catalan custom – attempting to drown the girl you love. Now it's his turn to suffer!

What a perfect day . . .

We stayed in the water for as long as we could bear. By the time we came out our lips had turned blue and the tips of Oriol's fingers were numb. In the evening we walked into Trewyss by ourselves and had 'feesh and cheep' (it's all he'll eat) on a bench by the harbour. It was dark by the time we left, and too dangerous to use the cliff path to get back to the cottage. So we walked in single file down the unlit narrow lanes, pressing ourselves into the prickly hedge every time a car or a caravan passed. There were bats flying around and the fields were singing with crickets. I walked in front because I knew the way, but I had to keep turning round to check that Oriol hadn't vanished like a dream.

'Talk to me,' I said into the darkness. 'I want to hear your voice.'

'I forget Engleesh words,' he replied wearily.

'Talk to me in Spanish then – in Catalan. Teach me something.'

'OK. I teach you numbers . . . '

So we spent the rest of the journey counting to ten in Catalan. The strange words are spinning round my head at the moment, but I'll probably have forgotten them by tomorrow. I've too many other things on my mind. Before we got back to the cottage we stopped to rest on the wooden bench at the top of the cliff path. It bears a small plaque, which reads, 'IN MEMORY OF WALTER CRANKS, WHO LOVED THIS SPOT'. No doubt the people who donated this seat imagined people gazing at the coastal scenery. I hope Walter Cranks, whoever he was, doesn't object to his bench being used for some rather passionate kissing! I feel as if I'm really getting the hang of it now – in fact, it's nowhere near as difficult as I imagined. Oriol's kisses are so fantastic they make my mouth feel really soft and sensitive. After a while my lips start to tingle round the edges. I know it sounds ridiculous, but it's true! I wonder if other girls experience the same sensation. Hannah's never mentioned it, but then she wasn't going out with her Newcastle United fan long enough to find out.

It's late now, and I'm lying in bed, supposedly getting an early night because we have to get up at six o'clock tomorrow morning for a show. I'm far too excited to sleep. Anyway, I promised I'd text-message Hannah to tell her how my meeting with Oriol had gone: 'how r u . . . in cwall . . . bn 4 swm with o . . . lots of xxing . . . 1 wk not enuf . . . in luv . . . e xx.' This text-messaging business is hopeless! I can't press the buttons quickly enough, so I keep entering the wrong letters. I could ring Hannah instead, I suppose, but I shouldn't really spend the money. Tomorrow I'll buy a stack of postcards and write to her instead. It'll be so much easier!

CHAPTER THIRTEEN

Postcards to Hannah:

Sunday

Hi! Everything is going brilliantly! Today we went to a festival near Tintagel – where King Arthur lived. Tried to explain about Camelot to Oriol, but he couldn't understand! Performed the caravan act in the rain – scary. Oriol nearly slipped off the roof (of the caravan I mean)! Went to pub tonight with everyone else – we want to be on our own, but it's not easy! O is soooo lovely. He's teaching me to speak Catalan. Love, E.

Monday
Dear H,

Time is going so fast! Too windy today so we couldn't use the crane. Watched Fizz do show instead. Oriol loves girls with nose studs so I've put mine back in. He says he doesn't want to go back to Spain. I wish he could stay or I could go with him. I'm already missing him and he hasn't even gone yet!! How are you? Have you heard from

Jason? Bye for now, Eleanor.

Tuesday

Only five more days! We did three shows today, I'm exhausted. Oriol and I have been passing juggling clubs - it's really hard but he's a good teacher. The trouble is, I keep looking at him, and not at the clubs! Rosa has invited us (me and Fizz) to come over to Barcelona next year to visit them. But I can't wait that long! Oriol and I are getting on so well, I can't imagine him not being here. How will I manage when he's gone?

Miss you heaps, Eleanor X.

Thursday

Hi there - me again! Sorry I didn't send you a card yesterday, too busy performing! Everything going really well between me and O. Must stop now and get ready to go out. Going for a pizza in Trewyss. Just the two of us for a change! At last. Wish we could stay here for ever. Keep smiling, E.

Friday

Thanks for your text messages. Only two more days of Oriol! It's not fair! Rained all day and the show was cancelled. It was meant to be our last performance, so it feels really weird now it's all over. I feel so sad. Oriol leaves v. early Sunday morning, counting down the hours now. I can't bear it. I realize that I love him – Really!

E.

P.S. Yes I do think you should phone Jason again! He might have lost your number or be ill. He deserves one more chance, but no more.

Saturday

I'm feeling too depressed to write. Will finish this after he's gone.

So, Saturday has arrived, as I knew it inevitably would. It's strange how the time passes and there's nothing anyone can do to stop it. I've never known a week slip by so quickly. When I woke up and realized it was the last full day, I just burst into tears! Still, I've got to make the most of it. By this time tomorrow Oriol will have left, and who knows when we shall see each other again? I must get up as fast as I can. Time for breakfast!

'Where is everybody?' I ask Rosa, who is making coffee in the kitchen.

'Fizz is sleepy, Oriol also. Dídac is . . . er . . . doing all the jobs for going . . . how you say?'

'Packing?'

'Yes, he is packing everything. Jordi has gone to buy feesh!'

'Fish?' I laugh. 'Fizz won't be very pleased!'

'No, we cook on the beach. Tonight. Special party!'

'Great! . . . Not that I want you to go. I don't. I'm really going to miss you. All of you.'

Rosa pads into the sitting room, wincing slightly as she lands on the sofa. Her ribs are still giving her

113

pain, but she is nearly ready to start performing again. Which is just as well, as I'm not going to be around to take her place. 'You are sad if you say goodbye with Oriol,' she says. 'You are his special friend, yes? You are his girl!'

'I suppose so.' I blush. 'I hope I'll see him again.'

'Of course!' Rosa smiles and stirs her coffee thoughtfully. 'But he must go to school, and you also. It is not easy. Oriol has many friends in Spain. You also. There are many Engleesh boys.'

'They're not as nice as Oriol, though,' I reply. Dear Rosa – I think she's trying to tell me that my holiday romance won't last as long as my tan. But she's wrong, I just know that she's wrong!

Fortunately, Jordi has just walked in to save us from an embarrassing silence. 'You like?' he asks, waving a bunch of silvery wet mackerel on a string.

'Yes, I do,' I laugh. 'But you'd better hide them before Fizz sees!'

We spend the morning wandering around the cottage, while the beach starts to fill up with holidaymakers, busily hammering their windbreaks into their favourite spots on the sand. This is probably their last day here too. Saturday is changeover day, and as it's the last weekend of the school holidays, there won't be many new arrivals. 'By tomorrow, we'll have the place to ourselves again,' rejoices Fizz. I hope Rosa understands that Fizz is only talking about the tourists!

At twelve noon Dad rings me on my mobile, as previously arranged, to give me his latest Alexander Report. There's not much news really. He and Julie have moved into the hospital flat and Julie has put some day clothes on for the first time since Alexander was born. Apparently this is a sign that she's cheering up. I try my hardest to sound interested and make all the right noises, but I can't really concentrate on the conversation. It all seems too far away.

'So what have you been doing?' Dad asks eventually.

'Nothing much. Been swimming. Been to a few festivals.' No, I did not tell him I've been suspended ten metres above the ground in a caravan, or that I've kissed a Spanish boy about a hundred times.

'Don't forget to write. And give me a ring sometimes – that's what the mobile's for,' he says.

'Yes, Dad. I will. I've got to go now, my lunch is ready.'

Of course, that was a lie. As if there would ever be 'lunch ready'! Oriol and I go to the beach shop and buy some crisps and a bar of chocolate. We eat them sitting on Walter Cranks's bench and then make our way along the cliff path in the opposite direction to Trewyss, towards the old lighthouse.

The weather's bright and windy, the fields are full of purple and yellow flowers and the waves are performing at their very best. Every so often we stop and admire them as they throw themselves recklessly against the rocks, the foam spraying upwards towards our faces, so that when we lick our lips they taste faintly of salt. Oriol tells me the Catalan words for everything – the sea, the sand, the sky, the birds – but none of them stick. All I will remember of this day is the feel of his hand in mine, his arm pressing lightly on my bare shoulder, his lips brushing against my neck, or his teeth gently nibbling my ear (which is a very odd sensation, I must say, and I'm not sure that I like it!).

The lighthouse is closed, but there is an ice-cream van in the car park, so we buy lollies and sit on the rocks. The sea has turned a deep emerald green.

'I am sad,' says Oriol, as he licks the end of his rocket and turns his tongue purple. 'I do not want to go.'

'I don't want you to go either.'

'I hate school. How you say – it sucks!'

'I'm really going to miss you,' I mumble, feeling the tears pricking in my eyes.

'School is stupid! My father he says I must do exams. Always exams. Why?' That was Oriol's longest sentence in English ever, and not a word of it was about *us*. Oh well, I mustn't read too much into that.

'I hope we can see each other again soon,' I venture hopefully.

'Yes. One day, you come to Spain?'

'Yes!'

He leans forward and gives me a really long, blackcurranty kiss. My orange lolly starts to drip onto my hand and down my wrist. The wasps that have been hovering around the rubbish bin will probably come and attack me now, but I don't care. I know it sounds ridiculous, but I can't remember ever feeling happier, or sadder, in my whole life.

We return to the cottage just as the beach is emptying. Jordi is already down there, and has got a small bonfire going. Fizz and Dídac clamber down the rocks, laden with bottles of wine, a basket of bread and a huge bowl of salad. Rosa follows carefully, carrying cushions and the famous bedspread that we seem to take everywhere. We huddle round the fire, the strong smell of barbecued mackerel sweeping up our nostrils.

'Disgusting,' says our resident vegetarian, but nobody takes any notice. Tonight we are doing things the Los Diabolos way.

'This is the final night of our stay,' announces Rosa. 'Tomorrow we go home and I am very sad. But now, we have big party and say adios!'

Jordi passes round the charred mackerel, tucked into pieces of pitta bread, stuffed with the oily salad. We eat in silence. Images of the past six weeks float through my head. A short while ago I knew nothing of these four people. Now I can't imagine them not being here. It's going to be horribly quiet once they've gone.

After we've eaten as much as we can manage, we rinse our fingers in a nearby rock pool. 'What shall we do now?' asks Fizz.

'Cricket!' jokes Dídac.

'No!' shouts Rosa, hitting him with a cushion. 'I never play cricket!'

Everyone laughs, and I blush. Then Dídac says something in Catalan and scampers back up the rocks to the cottage.

'What did he say?' I ask Fizz.

'He said he's just had a great idea. He's going to get his guitar.'

'Are we going to sing?'

'No,' replies Rosa. 'We dance the sardana.'

'What's the sardana?'

'Catalan dance, very easy . . .' she explains. 'This dance

all persons can do, a dance for the friends, for the family, to say we are all together . . . '

'I've seen it done in Barcelona,' says Fizz. 'Basically, you form a circle with your arms on each other's shoulders and shuffle about a bit.'

Dídac arrives back, waving his guitar, and urges us all to get to our feet. Oriol protests, but Jordi pulls him up. It's the first time I've seen him behave like a British teenager. I don't think he's too keen on traditional Catalan folk dancing, but there's no way he's getting out of it.

'When we dance the sardana, everyones put something in the centre,' insists Rosa. 'It says we share everything. This is because we are . . . how you say in Engleesh, Fizz? . . . comunidad.'

'Community.'

'OK, we are community, yes?'

Rosa puts down her sandals and Jordi flings in his T-shirt. I throw my bag in, and Fizz takes off a necklace. Oriol sighs with annoyance and grudgingly adds one of his trainers to the pile.

'Fizz, you stand here next to Jordi, and Nel next to Oriol – of course!' she adds with a twinkle in her dark brown eyes. We form a circle around the collection of items and I can't help but be reminded of a group of girls at a club, dancing round their handbags – not that that symbolizes a sense of community, it's just to make sure nothing gets nicked! Oriol shakes his head in dismay and gives me a grin as if to say, 'I'm sorry my mother's so embarrassing,' but Rosa doesn't embarrass me one bit. I'd rather dance the sardana with Los Diabolos than watch

Dad twirl around with my physics teacher any day! Dídac starts strumming the guitar, and the dance begins.

Fizz and I attempt to follow the strange tiny steps, criss-crossing our feet as if dancing a lazy Irish jig. Even though the movements are slow and gentle, it's not easy to dance in the sand, especially when the grown-ups amongst us have already drunk several bottles of wine. A group of lads who've come down for an evening swim stare at us for a few moments before picking up their surfboards and running down to the sea. The lady who runs the beach shop passes by, walking her dog. But we are not interested in audiences right now. We keep our gaze inwards to the circle. After a few minutes Dídac stops playing and joins us, humming the tune instead. Rosa and Jordi sing along and so would I, if I knew how it went.

I look round the circle as the sun begins to set: four pairs of dark eyes sparkling in the glow of the bonfire behind us . . . my mother's weird purple hair falling across her face . . . Dídac and Jordi with their long thin noses and the same drooping moustache . . . the feel of Oriol's bony shoulder under one hand, and Fizz's dungaree strap under the other. We are all Catalans, dancing the sardana – a dance for friends, for family. And I realize that I don't just love Oriol. I love them all . . . This is my real community, where my heart truly belongs. I so wish this moment never had to end . . .

But end it does – mainly because the circle has wandered drunkenly across the beach and I've fallen into the moat of an abandoned sandcastle. It would have to be me that broke the spell! Still, it's probably just as well, as things were getting very sloppy and sentimental back there!

'*Fantastico!*' cries Fizz. 'Now, who wants some pine-apple?' She cuts up the remains of her final juggling performance and hands the chunks round. The acid of the fruit makes my lips sting. It's almost dark now, and the sand is feeling cold underfoot.

'Nel – we go walk?' asks Oriol quietly.

'Yes! . . . Is that all right, Fizz?'

'Of course it is. Why are you asking me?'

Yes, why am I asking her? I'm not little Eleanor any longer, am I? Nel Sharpe doesn't ask her mother for permission to go for a walk with her boyfriend! . . . And yes, it *is* safe to use that word when describing Oriol. He really is my boyfriend. I'm sure that he thinks he is too!

The tide is out as far as can be. We walk down to the water's edge together and stare at the sinking sun – a huge orange blob hovering in the pink sky. We stand in silence for what feels like forever. I can't tell what Oriol is thinking about. Is he wishing he could stay here with me, or does he just not want to go back to school? I'm not going to ask, in case I don't like the reply. Oh no, now I'm crying. This is so uncool! A big fat tear rolls down my cheek just as Oriol turns to me and takes both my hands.

'Sorry,' I mutter, sniffing rather unattractively. 'Stupid. . .'

'Shhh, Nel. Do not cry,' he whispers quietly. 'I haf love for you.'

Oh my God! Did I really hear that? Did Oriol just tell me that he *loved* me? I quickly rack my brain for other possible interpretations of 'I haf love for you' but I can't

find any. He's kissing me now, and I'm feeling dizzy with
excitement. There are fireworks exploding in my chest. I
think I'm going to fall over.

Later
Just had the most amazing evening. Oriol told
me that he loves me, and would you believe it – I
didn't even have to say it first!

CHAPTER FOURTEEN

He's gone.

I've spent the last few days wandering around the cottage like a lost soul. The place is horribly quiet. Most of the holidaymakers have gone home, the beaches are empty and the temperature has plummeted – it's as if Jordi put the sun in the van and drove it back to Spain. I don't feel like doing any juggling practice, I have no interest in going to Trewyss and it's far too cold to swim. Everything I do, everywhere I go, reminds me of Oriol.

Fizz is obviously aware of my tragic state. This morning she insisted that I 'stop moping and get some fresh air into my lungs', so she dragged me off on a clifftop walk towards the lighthouse. As soon as I saw Walter Cranks's bench I started to cry and had to pretend that I'd twisted my ankle so that we could turn back. I don't want to go out. I want to lie on my bed and re-live every moment of that last evening, when we walked down to the sea and he kissed me in the sunset, as if we were starring in the most romantic movie ever made! 'I haf love for you' . . . That phrase keeps playing endlessly in my head. I know it sounds ridiculous to say things like 'Was it all a dream?' but that's exactly how it feels.

I'm not the only one in a strange mood. Since Los Diabolos left, Fizz has been rather snappy and irritable. Now that the summer festival season has come to an end, she needs to find some other way to earn money. Her latest plan is to make mirror frames out of seaweed, shells and rubbish washed up on the beach. No doubt we'll be spending our weekends collecting torn fishing nets, Coke bottles and bits of driftwood. They'll pile up in the cottage for months, stinking the place out, and she'll never get round to doing anything with them. Perhaps I can steer her in another direction – not sure what, though. She's not the type of person that has a proper job. I'm starting to wonder whether living in Cornwall is such a good idea. When I'm really honest with myself, I know I only suggested coming back here so that I could see Oriol again. Now he's gone, I don't really know why I'm here.

There's something else that's worrying me. When Los Diabolos drove away early on Sunday morning, Oriol and I didn't make any firm arrangements for staying in touch. Most of the time it doesn't seem to matter that we can't speak each other's language, but on this occasion it was a real nuisance. 'See you next year!' shouted Fizz gaily, as the van clattered away. Next year? I can't possibly wait that long!

I've decided to phone Hannah on my mobile. I know I'm only meant to use it for contacting Dad, but I've got to talk to somebody who understands how I feel.

'I got your postcard this morning. I couldn't believe it!' screams Hannah immediately. 'He actually said he *loved* you – that is so amazing!'

'But I didn't tell him that I loved him too,' I wail in reply. 'I was so shocked when he said it, I couldn't speak! And then we got into a major kissing session and after that I couldn't find the right moment. I need to let him know or he might think I don't care about him!'

'Of course he knows you care! Oh, Eleanor, you are so lucky!'

'No I'm not! I might never even see him again! I can't ring him. Even if I could afford it, we'd never be able to understand each other.'

'You'll have to do a crash course in Spanish then!' laughs Hannah, trying to joke me out of my despair. But it's not working.

'I wish we could chat properly,' I groan. 'I'm so lonely here. I really miss you.'

'I miss you too . . . Can't you talk about it to your mum?'

'Not really. She wouldn't understand . . .'

'Well, you mustn't start worrying, I'm sure everything is absolutely fine,' Hannah assures me cheerfully. 'He's probably missing you like crazy. I mean, he wouldn't have said he loved you if he hadn't meant it.'

'No, I suppose not,' I reply. 'I'm going to try not to think about it too much. Guess what, it's my first day at the new school tomorrow. I'm dreading it.'

'Oh, you'll be fine,' says Hannah. 'You'll make heaps of new friends. It's me you should be feeling sorry for. I don't know how I'm going to manage without you.'

'It's going to be really weird—' Suddenly the phone conks out – I must remember to keep re-charging my battery! Aaagh!

★ ★ ★

So, today is my first day at Northquay Comprehensive. I'm feeling a bit nervous, and didn't sleep very well last night. Fizz said she would drive me there this morning, but if she doesn't wake up soon, we'll be late. I go into her room, draw open the curtains and shake her gently by the shoulders.

'Wha . . . ?' she grunts, turning away and pulling the pillow over her head.

'You're taking me to school, remember?'

She lets out a long sleepy groan and I can't help but think of Dad, who gets up at 6.30 every morning to have a shower and shave. He wakes me up with a cup of tea at seven o'clock sharp and spends the next hour giving me time-checks. 'Seven minutes past, Eleanor, you should be up by now . . . Thirteen minutes past, don't forget it's games today . . . Eighteen minutes past . . . How do you want your egg?'

We have an egg every morning, with two slices of wholemeal toast and fresh orange juice. He insists that a cooked breakfast helps to stimulate the brain cells, or something like that. Every morning is the same, and by half term the routine is usually driving me mad. But right now I'd love to come downstairs and see Dad in the kitchen, smelling of shaving foam, buttering the toast. There's no milk so I eat a bowl of dry cornflakes, washed down with a glass of water. I can't see my brain cells doing much with that!

'Fizz! It's twenty-five to nine!'

'I'm coming!' she shouts back, thumping down the stairs, looking like a hideous monster disturbed from her lair.

125

I virtually drag Fizz to the car and put the keys in the ignition. She takes the winding back route, avoiding the more direct A-road, because she claims it will be quicker. As we turn right at the riding stables, the lane gets narrower and narrower and I'm not sure Fizz knows exactly where she's going. We slow down for a line of pony trekkers, and then get stuck behind a tractor . . .

'Can't you overtake? We're late!'

'Keep calm, Nel, it can't be far now . . . You'll have to catch the school bus tomorrow. I'm not having this panic every morning, it's bad for my nerves.'

It's not doing my nerves any good, either. I'd much rather take the bus – at least I won't have to drag the driver out of bed first!

Northquay Comprehensive is about eight miles from the cottage, just outside Northquay itself, a large seaside town, famous for its surf beaches. Fizz says the place is a dump – 'a beauty spot wrecked by tourists' is how she'd describe it if she were writing the holiday brochures. Just the mention of Northquay makes her shudder and screw up her nose. No doubt she imagines that its main school is full of amusement arcades and bingo halls too, but it looks pretty ordinary to me.

'Are you going to come in?'

'Whatever for?' Fizz drives through the school gates. I don't know whether she didn't spot the 'STAFF AND DELIVERIES ONLY' sign, or whether she's deliberately ignoring it.

On second thoughts, it might be safer to go in by myself. Who knows what she might say to the head teacher while she's in this rebellious mood?

'Nel Sharpe? . . . Sharpe . . . Sharpe . . . No, I haven't got that name down here,' says the school secretary, flicking through a pile of papers.

'Actually, you've probably got me down as Eleanor Sharratt.'

'Ah, yes . . . E. Sharratt . . . Nine W. You're rather late. Registration is at eight forty-five a.m. every morning. I'll have to find out where you're supposed to be for first period . . .'

Thanks, Fizz – this is just the sort of start I didn't want.

Ten minutes later I'm shown into a science lab full of students performing experiments with raw potatoes. There's quite a lot of low-level talking going on, but it stops when they notice me. The teacher, whose name I've just been told and promptly forgotten, takes me up to the only girl who hasn't got a partner.

'Lowenna – this is Eleanor Sharratt,' says Miss Thingamabob. 'She's going to be with us for the autumn term.'

'Actually, my name's Nel,' I mumble nervously. This is strange. It looks as if I'm going to be Nel Sharratt here. I'm not sure if I can cope with three versions of myself!

'Hi,' grins a rather hefty girl who's as tall as me, but must weigh at least three stone more. She has auburn hair, which looks dyed, small blue eyes and a square chin. Lowenna isn't wearing a lab coat, and her shirt and skirt are a rather loose interpretation of the uniform rules. Fizz would no doubt approve. 'What on earth have you come here for?' asks Lowenna. 'This place is crap.'

'I'm staying with my mother.'

'Oh, right. Your parents split up or something?'

'Yes, but years ago.'

'Where's she live then, your mum?'

'Pentonwarra Bay. Just outside Trewyss.'

'Girls! Get on with your experiment, please. You can chat later.'

Lowenna pulls a face behind the teacher's back and writes the date on her worksheet. It's all she does for the rest of the lesson. I end up doing all the actual experimenting while Lowenna asks me endless questions about myself. By lunchtime I feel as if she knows even more about me than Hannah. She can't believe that I'd rather be in Cornwall than in some Midlands city full of trendy shops, bars and clubs. We don't seem to have a single thing in common, but she's decided to adopt me as her friend. And as nobody else has stepped forward with an alternative offer, I've no choice but to accept.

'So, can you do circus stuff, too?' she quizzes me as we queue up for lunch.

'Well, I can juggle, and ride a unicycle . . . And this summer I took part in a flying caravan stunt.'

'No way!' gasps Lowenna admiringly.

Before I know it, I'm telling her all about Los Diabolos and Oriol, 'my Spanish boyfriend'. She's just split up from her boyfriend, or so she tells me. It's slightly worrying that she doesn't seem to have any other friends, apart from a couple of tarty-looking girls in the year above, who've been giving me some rather aggressive looks.

'Why don't you come into Northquay with me at the weekend?' Lowenna offers as we walk from French to RE.

'OK. I'll ask my mum, see what she says . . . '

These first four days of school have been very strange. Lessons are pretty much the same, but I can't get used to the fact that I don't know the names of most people in my form. My home life is pretty peculiar too. Fizz seems to have forgotten that I'm living here. She's still asleep when I leave the house in the morning and she's out when I come home. I've had to make my own tea – alternating between beans on toast and cheese sand-wiches – and yesterday I had to put on a load of washing because I'd run out of school blouses. The last few evenings have been really boring. There's nobody to chat to, no television to watch, and if I have to listen to my CDs one more time, I shall go mad. Fizz doesn't come home until really late and last night she didn't come back at all! Dad would have a blue fit if he knew I was in the cottage on my own. But there are some compensations – Fizz hasn't nagged me about homework, or insisted on correcting the spelling in my latest essay, or told me it's 'about time I was in bed' – which is what Dad does *all* the time.

It's Friday night and, surprise, surprise, I'm on my own again. I've been staring at the phone for the last half-hour, trying to resist the temptation to call Oriol. All I want to do is hear his voice! But I'm not allowed and I'd better not risk it. The other day I asked Fizz if I could ring Barcelona – 'just for thirty seconds, I'll only say hello!' – but she went ballistic. Apparently, she is com-pletely broke and has a huge overdraft (not that it stops her going off to the pub every night). But not to worry

– I'm about to put Plan B into action. Hannah text-messaged me with the brilliant idea that I should write Oriol a letter and get Fizz to translate it into Spanish. It's a bit embarrassing, having to ask your mum to rewrite your love letters, but it's my only hope of getting in touch with him.

So this is what I'm doing with the rest of my lonely evening. It takes me about two hours to decide what to say and the best way to say it. I'm quite pleased with what I've written. It's friendly and affectionate, but not too sloppy. I haven't put 'I love you too' because he'll understand that in English. I can just add it as a PS when Fizz gives me back the Spanish version.

By the time Fizz gets home it's well past midnight, and I've fallen asleep on the sofa, waiting for her to return.

'I thought you'd be in bed,' she says vaguely. 'God, I'm starving!'

I rouse myself, grab the letter and follow her into the kitchen. 'Please! It's not too much to translate. I kept it short!' I beg, waving it in her face.

'No, Nel!' Fizz replies irritably. 'I can't write Spanish.' I realize – too late – that I've picked the wrong moment to ask. Fizz is tired, she's had too much to drink and now she's annoyed because I used up the last of the bread. 'Why is there never anything to eat in this house?' she moans.

Because you never go to the shops, I reply in my head, but now is not the time to argue. 'Please translate my letter. You're brilliant at Spanish, you know you are!' I insist.

'No, I'm not. I've never had a proper lesson in my life. I don't know how to spell half the words.'

'Use your dictionary,' I persist. 'Please! I can't do it

130

without your help. You won't let me ring — how else are we supposed to keep in touch?'

'Leave it on the dining table,' she says wearily. 'I'll try and do it over the weekend. Now let me get to bed!'

It's Saturday morning — a whole week has gone by since Oriol told me he loved me! It's eleven and Fizz is still fast asleep, so I've left her a note.

Hi, Fizz! Hope you're feeling OK. I've bought some bread and there's orange juice in the fridge. Gone to Northquay with Lowenna — girl from school. Hope you have a good day. If by any chance you get round to translating my letter, I'd be really really grateful! Thanks in advance. Love you lots, Nel XXXXXXXXX

That should do the trick.

Fizz is right about Northquay — it's a dump. The main street is a tatty mixture of fast food outlets, noisy pubs and discount stores selling plastic beach equipment. Several shops have closed down and now that the holidaymakers have gone home the place looks rather sorry for itself. The grey clouds overhead and the thin film of drizzle only add to the forlorn atmosphere. Or maybe it's just me — I'm not in the right mood for this trip. We arrived here about half an hour ago and Lowenna immediately made a beeline for the biggest, noisiest amusement arcade she could find. I've lost count of the number of coins she's fed into the fruit machines and she's hardly won a thing. *This is not my idea of fun.*

'Aren't you going to play?' she shouts incredulously.

'No thanks, I'm going outside for a bit. This place is giving me a headache.'

School uniform is very deceptive, isn't it? It makes people look the same, when in fact they are quite different. Today Lowenna is wearing designer jogging bottoms, expensive trainers and a tight-fitting lycra T-shirt. If it wasn't for her bulging stomach and fat thighs, you'd think she'd just come out of the gym (sorry, that was a really bitchy thing to say, wasn't it). In contrast, I am a long thin hippie, wearing my favourite tie-dye swirly skirt that Dad hates so much, and a white embroidered cotton top. Nobody would believe for a moment that the two of us were meant to be friends.

After standing on the pavement for twenty minutes wondering to myself why on earth I agreed to come here, I go back into the arcade to find Lowenna thrashing the life out of the Grand Prix racing machine.

'Shall we check out the beach?' I shout above the clanging, chinking, thumping din.

'Yeah, I've spent all my money anyway.' Lowenna swings her car around the track at top speed and crashes into the barrier. GAME OVER flashes across the screen. 'Hey, Nellie, can you buy me a burger?'

We make our way down a twisty side street, where there are several hippy shops I would have loved to explore, but Lowenna leads me firmly past them towards the surf shops – or rather 'surf shacks' – on the promenade. This is where the really cool dudes hang out, comparing the depth of their tan and the size of their surfboards. All the men seem to have shoulder-length blond hair, bleached by the sun (or so they'd have us think), and wear their wet-suits round their waists, revealing firm six pack abdomens and hairless muscular chests. They must be doing this to show off, because it's no way warm enough to be walking around like that! And why am I not drooling over these rejects from an Australian soap opera? Last year my knees would have gone all trembly just passing one of these places, but I suppose my tastes have changed. I'm more into the dark, sultry type now, preferably from Catalonia and called Oriol.

'So, who do you normally hang around with?' I ask Lowenna as we sit on the wall, eating the burgers that she rather cleverly got me to pay for.

'Oh, there's quite a gang of us usually,' she claims. 'We meet outside the bingo hall. Come on, let's go find them.'

I'm not sure I want to hang around with a load of trendy types, who no doubt smoke and swear at the tops of their voices (another bitchy comment – and, of course, Oriol smokes). However, I let Lowenna lead me back to the town centre. To my relief, none of her 'gang' are there – if they exist at all – so we sit down on the steps off the bingo hall and wait. I can't remember being more bored in my entire life, although I probably have.

'Look over there!' says Lowenna, pointing. 'What idiot would dress up as a penguin for a living?'

A penguin? I peer across the road and, sure enough, there's a human-size penguin, playing the saxophone and dancing to a small crowd. It must be Wolfgang or Oskar. There can't be any other saxophone-playing penguins working in Cornwall, can there?

'I know him!' I cry, crossing the road without look-ing as carefully as I should. Lowenna follows at a slower pace. I think she's a bit embarrassed to be seen with any-one who is friends with a penguin, but that's her problem. As the song finishes, the crowd claps weakly and moves on. Only two people put any money on the cloth at the penguin's feet. Some people are so mean!

'Hello! It's me – Nel. Fizz's daughter!' I wave franti-cally at the pair of eyes peeking out through the penguin's beak. 'Which one are you?'

'Wolfgang! Hey, how you doing?'

'Fine . . . Where's Oskar?'

'Long story,' Wolfgang replies wearily. 'Let us drink some tea and I'll tell you all about it.'

We're now sitting in a noisy café, which smells of bacon and chip fat, drinking stewed tea out of polystyrene cups. I'm sure it's not up to German catering standards, but Wolfgang doesn't seem to mind. In fact, he's surprisingly pleased to see me. Lowenna, I'm relieved to say, has decided to go to Woolworths to get a magazine.

'Oskar has gone back to Frankfurt,' Wolfgang explains sadly. 'He has a good job there. I do not blame him. But I am left here on my own. It is not easy. One penguin is not so funny.' Why is it that every German I've ever met can speak perfect English?

'Where are you staying?'

'In a youth hostel. I should go back to Germany, I sup-pose, but I would rather stay here . . . I like England.'

'You could come and stay with us!' Wolfgang looks rather pathetic in his penguin costume, like a stray

134

animal in need of adoption. 'Fizz won't mind, she loves having visitors.'

So that is why Lowenna and I are riding the bus back to Trewyss in the company of a penguin with a large rucksack and a saxophone case. I don't think this is quite how Lowenna imagined the day turning out, but I couldn't be happier. Well, actually, I could be happier – I could be sitting on the bus with Oriol, but you know what I mean. And speaking of Oriol, I do hope Fizz has translated my letter!

CHAPTER FIFTEEN

Isn't it amazing how your whole life can change in two weeks? Well, that's a bit of an exaggeration, but let's say life with Fizz has changed *considerably*, and not for the better. The problem? That poor, forlorn penguin that I rescued from Northquay. Why, oh why didn't I leave him outside the bingo hall to fend for himself? Why did I bring him back to the sanctuary of the cottage so that he and my mother could fall madly in love?

Yes, Cupid has struck. I'm not sure exactly when it started because I've been at school, but about a week ago they went to the pub without me (as usual) returning extremely late and rather drunk. When I got up the next morning Wolfgang wasn't asleep on the sofa . . . Need I say more? Let me tell you, seeing two middle-aged people snogging is not a pretty sight. It is so embarrassing walking around Trewyss harbour with them wrapped around each other like two octopuses, gazing into each other's eyes and constantly giving each other affectionate pecks. It doesn't seem to occur to them that I am witness to all this revolting behaviour – unless they're doing it deliberately so that I'll go up to my bedroom and leave them to slobber all over each other in peace.

You're probably wondering why I'm being so negative about all this. Why am I not rejoicing that my mother has found herself a boyfriend? Don't I want her to be happy? Well, of course I do, but Wolfgang is so not right for her! She *thinks* she's happy with him, but deep inside she can't be. I mean, he's just not her type!

Let me give you a few examples. Since Wolfgang arrived the cottage has been tidied up and cleaned from top to bottom. Weird or what? The enormous pile of dirty clothes that has been littering the bathroom all summer has been washed, dried, ironed and put away in Fizz's wardrobe. Unheard of! The kitchen cupboards are stocked high with tins and packets, the fridge is bursting with smoked cheese, garlic sausage (yes, meat!), coleslaw and tubs of lumpy natural yoghurt. All very German and not the sort of stuff Fizz likes. Wolfgang cooks the evening meal, making a great display in the kitchen as if he's some celebrity chef on the television. But then they expect me to wash up (Fizz has never washed up unless she's run out of plates) while they collapse on each other in the sitting room – I can hear their squelchy kisses from the next room!

I suppose I should be grateful. I was getting rather fed up with having to cook my tea and iron my school uniform. But if somebody's going to look after me properly I want it to be either Dad or Fizz. I don't want another father. This Wolfgang business has made me realize that I'm happy enough with the one I've got.

I don't get it. Fizz is thirty-eight and Wolfgang is only twenty-seven. She's nearly old enough to be his mother! I can just about see why she'd fancy him – he's blond and slim, with suspiciously even features that make him look like a plastic Action Man figure. But why is he interested in Fizz? She's just not his type – she's got that typical hippie look, un-ironed and unwashed. Well, she used to have. Now they have a bath together every night! They spend hours in the bathroom, filling it with perfumed candles and South American flute music. The other night I got so desperate I had to pee in the back garden! It wouldn't surprise me one bit if Fizz cut off her dreadlocks, put blonde highlights in her hair and started wearing little black dresses. Something weird is going on, I'm sure of it. Wolfgang's always saying how much he loves England – perhaps he wants to trick Fizz into marrying him so that he can have a British passport! I've seen films about that – true, they usually involve Russians or people wanting to be Americans, but it could be what's happening here. I'd like to warn Fizz, but she's never on her own. She wouldn't listen to me anyway. At the moment we're not exactly what you'd call 'getting on'.

I suppose the thing that's *really* annoyed me is that Fizz hasn't translated my letter to Oriol. I patiently left it on the dining table for the first three days, but it was ignored. Then I started asking her to do it, using the sweetest tones I could muster. I fetched the dictionary, the paper, the pen, a cup of raspberry-leaf tea, a glass of wine – anything to put her in the right mood. She kept promising to get round to it, but she never did. Then this 'thing' with Wolfgang started and since then she's been too busy snogging. A few days ago we had a horrible row about it, in which she accused me of 'nagging'!

'You're just selfish!' I screamed back. 'You *never* do anything for me. All you think about is yourself!'

'Well, I'm not going to treat you like a five-year-old, if that's what you want!' she shouted back. 'You know your trouble, Nel? You've been spoilt! You're not Daddy's little princess here, so you'd better get used to it!'

'Dad doesn't treat me like a princess! He just looks after me, like any normal parent! You don't even know what parents are meant to do! You've no idea how to be a mum!'

'You'd better go back to Derbyshire then!' shouted Fizz. 'If your life there is so bloody wonderful.'

'I will!'

'Good! But remember, they've got another baby to look after now. You're going to have to share. Something you don't seem to be very good at.'

Ouch! That last remark struck right where it hurt. I stormed up to my bedroom and we haven't spoken since.

I've been seriously tempted to pack my bags and return to Dad's, but something's stopping me. I know he would come and get me like a shot if he knew what was going on here, but once I was home it would cause all sorts of extra problems. I'd have to go back to my old school, which would mean living in our house. But Dad and Julie are still staying at the hospital flat, and although Alexander is out of his incubator and breathing by himself, it will be several weeks before he's well enough to leave the hospital. Dad would have to leave the flat to look after me and that would upset Julie. She's got this post natal depression and I don't want to get the blame for making it any worse. So I'm stuck here for the time being, with Fizz and the penguin.

It's Saturday afternoon and I'm sitting on my bed, staring out of my window at the triangle of grey sea merging into the cloudy sky. Downstairs, Fizz and Wolfgang are working out a new double act. Wolfgang dismissed Fizz's mirror frame idea – one thing we actually agree on – and declared that the two of them should form a new musical juggling duo, performing in indoor shopping centres throughout the winter months. Ever eager to wear his stupid penguin costume, he has suggested that Fizz dresses up as a polar bear and juggles Christmas parcels, while he plays carols on the saxophone. Normally my mother would never do a show as naff as that, but this new Fizz thinks it's a fantastic idea! I pointed out that polar bears are only found in the North Pole and penguins only in the South and that this could mislead children in the audience.

'We are being creative here, Nel. We do not need your negative input,' Wolfgang sneered in his clipped accent. 'Why don't you go and see some friends?'

I'd love to, if I had any to see. There's Lowenna, of course, but I don't like her very much. I've discovered that hardly anybody else in the school does either. She's loud, aggressive and rude to the teachers. It was a really bad mistake to allow myself to be adopted by her. Now everyone thinks I'm just like her, so they don't want anything to do with me. The only way I could get rid of her would be by having a serious row in a very public place, but I'd rather have her as my friend than my enemy. She

140

has links with a few nasty girls in the year above who have a reputation for bullying other kids. I'm sure there are nice people at Northquay Comprehensive, but I've no chance of making friends with them – not now. And anyway, I'll probably be gone by Christmas, so what's the point?

I am *so miserable*. I've text-messaged Hannah twice already today, but she hasn't replied. I expect she's out with her other friends, eyeing up the boys at the sports hall or shopping for clothes in the town centre. I miss her so much. I miss my Eleanor self too. Eleanor normally does trampolining on Saturday afternoons – she's good at trampolining. She can somersault and do the 'swivel-hips' and this term her teacher was going to enter her in a competition. As for Nel, she's just moping about in her cold, damp bedroom, feeling sorry for herself.

I take out the juggling balls that Oriol gave me and throw them into the air. They are bright and sparkly, like tiny planets spinning through space. Suddenly I realize that this is my life – juggling between my two parents, my two homes, my two selves, Eleanor and Nel. First one, then the other, then the first one again, back and forth, back and forth. And this third ball – this is Oriol, flying in between them. Where is he right now? What's he doing? I bet he's not sulking in his bedroom, wondering about me. It's been three weeks since I last saw him and his image is starting to fade from my memory. I haven't even got a photo of him. I wish he'd call, or send me a card, but I've heard nothing. How long does it take for letters to reach Spain? I took back the letter and posted it as it was, in English. Oriol might be able to understand some of it, or maybe Rosa will be able to translate it for him. Who knows? One thing's for certain, if I never hear from Oriol again, it will be all Fizz's fault.

CHAPTER SIXTEEN

It's my birthday! Fourteen today. I stretch out my long thin limbs and touch the edge of the bed with my toes, as if to test whether I've grown overnight. I haven't, of course – not that I can tell, anyway. I've a feeling I'm not going to grow upward any more, just outwards. There is one area where I would like to see a bit of outward growth – two areas actually, if you get my meaning! Perhaps fourteen is the year when I'm going to 'blossom' and get a bit of shape to my body. I know it's fashionable to look as if you're on a starvation diet, but I'm a bit too thin . . . my body is nothing but a long straight tube. Still, there's no time for this sort of contemplation, I've got to get up and begin my Special Day!

I drag on my school uniform and knock hopefully on Fizz's bedroom door. There is no reply. She and the penguin are still fast asleep, wrapped in each other's arms. It makes me want to throw up. So, no birthday breakfast treat for me then? No chocolate croissants and freshly squeezed orange juice? It would appear not. I walk down the stairs, wondering whether there were any secret goings-on after I went to bed last night. But the sitting room is as I left it – cold, damp and tidy in a very un-Fizz sort of way.

There are no brightly wrapped parcels lurking around, no balloons, no 'HAPPY BIRTHDAY' banners, no coloured envelopes on the doormat. Then I remember that the postman doesn't arrive until after I've left for school. As far as I know, Dad didn't send anything in advance. I haven't got the date wrong, have I? It *is* 4 October, isn't it?

I go to the kitchen and eat a miserable bowl of muesli. I don't feel anything like fourteen, I feel about five. I want to cry. It's my birthday and everyone has forgotten! Or have they? *Maybe* it's like one of those episodes on children's TV. You know – the one where it's somebody's birthday and they're feeling miserable because they think nobody's remembered. Then, at the end, all their friends leap out and say 'Surprise! Surprise!' and there's a massive party. Maybe Fizz and the penguin were pretending to be asleep and are about to run downstairs with a huge glittery parcel. Maybe I'm going to step outside the cottage and a brass band will strike up 'Happy Birthday!' And maybe not.

So, what am I going to do on my Special Day, then? Nothing has been discussed, nothing has been arranged (which makes me think it just might be a surprise). I don't know why I should be feeling upset. I don't want to spend my birthday with Fizz and the penguin anyway. The only person I really want to spend my birthday with is Oriol and he's in Spain. So unless somebody has bought me a plane ticket to Barcelona, which seems unlikely, I'm going to be spending my fourteenth birthday at Northquay Comprehensive doing (quick look at my timetable here) double maths, French, double geography and R.E. Wonderful . . .

And here I am, listening to Madame Garside drone on about the imperfect tense while Lowenna doodles on her exercise book and whispers all about her plans for this evening. At least she's keen to go out and celebrate my birthday. She wants us to go to McDonald's and then to see a horror film, which is an eighteen certificate. I've already pointed out that this is my four-teenth birthday, not my eighteenth, and although we are both tall for our age, I don't think we'll get in. But Lowenna claims she's been to hundreds of eighteens and that it will be 'a piece of p★★★'. I've also told her that I don't like horror movies because they give me night-mares, but this doesn't seem to have registered in Lowenna's tiny brain.

'Horror films aren't scary, they're funny!' she insists. 'You can't just sit at home all evening.'

'Fizz might have organized a surprise for me.'

'You said this morning she'd forgotten.'

'I know . . . But she's never forgotten before.'

'When it's my birthday, my brothers and sisters wake me up by singing in my ears. And I have all my presents before breakfast! Last year I got a telly and a computer.'

'Well, Fizz isn't like other people. She does things her own way.'

'Didn't your dad send you nothing either?'

'Not yet. But the post hadn't arrived.'

'Your mum and dad are really slack. Don't they care about you at all?'

'It's not that, it's—'

'Nel and Lowenna, one more word from either of you

145

and you'll be in lunchtime detention!' Madame Garside (why do we call her 'Madame', she's not French!) shoots us a threatening look.

'That ent fair, miss, it's her birthday!' protests Lowenna. 'You can't give detentions on people's birth-days!'

'I'll decide who I'm giving detentions to, not you. For that, you can both come and see me at twelve-thirty.'

'No way!'

'Yes, Lowenna. I said "one more word" and you've already said several.'

'Cow . . .' mutters Lowenna under her breath.

So, now I'm spending my birthday lunchtime in detention! Lowenna can't believe that it's the first deten-tion I've *ever* had – she gets at least one a week. The temptation to walk out of the school gates is over-whelming. The end of Northquay beach is only fifteen minutes' walk away . . . If I could find a boat, I'd sail to Barcelona and never come back. But would I be any more welcome there? It's two weeks now since I sent the letter to Oriol and he hasn't replied yet. Maybe I sent it to the wrong address. I copied it out of Fizz's book, but her handwriting's so messy, I might have misread the number of their apartment.

'I'm not staying in this dump another second,' says Lowenna as the bell for afternoon lessons rings. 'We'll get our mark and then run for it.'

'But what if we're caught?'

'We won't be. Come on! You can't spend your birth-day at school!'

After registration Lowenna grabs me by the arm and

146

we run out of a side door, sneaking through a gap in the bushes on the edge of the football pitch and then through a hole in the fence. Lowenna seems to know the route like the back of her hand. 'If anyone stops and asks, we're doing a geography project, OK?' She removes her school top and stuffs it into her bag. 'Take your jumper off or do your coat up . . . Right. First job is to get you a decent birthday present.'

I note nervously that Lowenna did not use the word 'buy'. 'You're not planning to nick something, are you?' I reply, trying not to sound too shocked.

'Don't be such a baby! How will we get into an eighteen if you're wearing school uniform.'

'I don't particularly want to go to the cinema.'

'Then where *do* you want to go?'

'Barcelona.'

'Where's that then?'

'Spain.'

'Oh right, then, I'll nick you a bikini instead,' says Lowenna sarcastically, as she marches me into the town centre. 'Cheer up. We're going to have a good time, you and me. I'm going to give the best birthday ever, all right?'

Oh dear, this is getting very awkward. The conventional, obedient, well-behaved Eleanor Sharratt is feeling extremely anxious. She has never had a detention, or skipped school, and she's certainly never been involved in any shoplifting. She is trying to tell Nel Sharpe to go back to the cottage now before anything really bad happens. But Nel doesn't want to listen. She is busy distracting the only assistant in Miss Teen, asking her if she has a certain pair of trousers in size eight, while Lowenna is stuffing two halter-neck tops and a denim skirt into her school bag.

'Do you have the navy ones in size eight too?' I ask, flashing my baby blue eyes.

Suddenly there is the sound of the alarm as Lowenna dashes out of the shop. I'm meant to stay there and act the innocent, but the Eleanor Sharratt part of me panics and starts to run. 'Oi, come back! We'll get you! You're on camera!' shouts the girl after Eleanor – or is it Nel? – who's pounding along the high street, dodging in and out of startled shoppers.

Lowenna was only a few paces in front, but has suddenly vanished. I glance round, already breathless. The assistant has gone back into the shop – to call the police, no doubt. How long before they're behind me, chasing me, hunting me down? The plan was to meet Lowenna by Woody's Surf Shack, but now I've forgotten how to get there. My heart's pounding, I'm sweating, I run across the road, down some steps. These stupid shoes . . . I should be wearing trainers. People are looking at me. I know what they're thinking – they know I'm a thief . . . Got to get away . . . Run faster, faster . . . round the corner, down a cobbled alley. I look behind – there's nobody chasing me but I've got to keep running. An old man comes out of his house and stops in the street. I dart to one side to avoid him, twist my ankle and fall . . .

'You all right, dearie?' he says, but I can't look at him. I'm too ashamed. I get up: my foot's killing me – I can hardly walk, but I've got to run, got to get to the promenade . . .

'You idiot! What the hell did you do that for?' screams Lowenna, who has suddenly appeared out of nowhere and is dragging me into the beach toilets.

'Sorry, I just panicked! . . . Ouch! My foot really hurts . . .'

'I told you to stay there! Now they'll have you on their stupid cameras.'

'I know. They'll have you too . . .'

'No they won't. Not so they can recognize me, anyway. I know how to keep my face out of sight. Why d'yer think I been wearing this cap?' Lowenna takes it off and puts it in her pocket. Then she takes out a creased grey sweatshirt she uses for hockey and squeezes it over my head. 'They won't be looking for anyone wearing this. You are such an idiot.'

'I'm sorry . . . Will they call the police?'

'Probably.'

'I can't believe this! I've never done anything like this before!'

'We'll have to dump the stuff,' says Lowenna, throwing out the soggy paper towels from a bin and putting the stolen clothes underneath. 'Pity – this skirt is really nice . . .'

'What will my dad say if he finds out? Or Fizz?'

'Look, the chances are they won't find us. But we'll have to keep out of the way till the shops are shut.'

'I need to go home – my ankle really hurts.'

'You can't go home yet, you're meant to be at school, remember?'

'OK, but I need to sit down!'

★ ★ ★

149

So here we are, in the cinema watching some revolting horror movie for the third time round. Correction: Lowenna is watching it, her mouth permanently open to receive the handfuls of popcorn she is shovelling in. I've spent most of the film with my hands in front of my eyes. I don't know how we got in, but we did. The place is virtually empty, so I suppose they're glad of the custom. After the first showing Lowenna wanted to go the pub, but I refused. Some birthday, eh? My ankle is swollen and bruised – it still hurts when I put weight on it. It must be dark. Surely they've stopped searching for us by now. I've no idea what the time is. We've probably missed the last bus home.

We have – by about two hours! That's Cornwall for you. It's gone ten o'clock and we're stuck in Northquay. There's no way I could make the eight-mile walk. Lowenna is trying to persuade me to hitch, but I've had enough danger for one day.

'If only we had some money, we could get a taxi,' I sigh as we wander down the main street like two lost souls. In my mind's eye I can see my cash card sitting on the chest of drawers in my bedroom.

'That's the answer,' says Lowenna. 'We'll get a taxi, he can drop me off at the end of the lane and when you get near your mum's place – not too near, mind you – ask him to stop and then make a run for it!'

'I can't do that.'

''Course you can. People do it all the time.'

'For a start, it's against the law, and second, I can't run!'

'But it'll cost a fortune!'

'I've got some money indoors. I'll ask him to wait.'

'You are such a goody-goody!' laughs Lowenna as we walk into a taxi place near the bingo hall. There's a long queue of old ladies and we have to wait half an hour before there's a taxi available for us. It's gone eleven o'clock, and I'm starting to feel more than a bit nervous about the reception I'm going to get once I arrive home. Lowenna says her mum will go mad at her, but she doesn't care. Even if she tries to ground her, she won't take any notice. 'They know they can't touch me,' Lowenna boasts. 'I'm what they call "out of control".'

By the time the taxi has dropped Lowenna off at her farm and we've snaked our way back towards the cottage, it's horribly late. I explain the situation to the driver and go round to the back door. It's still open – actually, I don't think Fizz ever locks it.

'Nel! Where have you been?' Fizz says angrily, leaping up from the sofa. 'I've been trying to call you on your mobile for hours – why did you switch it off?'

'I've just got to get some money for the taxi,' I mutter, limping over to my bag and out to the waiting taxi-driver.

'We've been waiting for you all evening!' says Wolfgang as I walk back through the door.

'That makes a change!'

'Nel, you don't understand. We've been worried. We nearly called the police!'

The mention of the word 'police' makes me start with fright. 'I just went out, that's all.'

'But it's your birthday.'

'Oh yes, my birthday!' I shout sarcastically. 'Have I missed some party then? Organized a big surprise, had you?'

'We were going to take you out for a meal, as it happens. Wolfgang made you a beautiful birthday cake.'

'I've already eaten. You'd better feed it to the seagulls.'

'Nel, that's so rude!'

'It doesn't matter about the cake, darling,' soothes Wolfgang. 'The problem is that Nel went off by herself and she did not tell us.'

'You do it all the time! You're always leaving me on my own in the house.'

'Yes, but we're adults,' says Fizz.

'I thought you didn't want to treat me like a five-year-old any more. I thought you wanted me to be more grown-up. Changed your mind, have you?'

'Nel, stop this!'

'You must not shout at your mother!' says Wolfgang, shouting at me.

'Mother? She's not my mother! Mothers don't forget their own daughter's birthday! They don't spend all day in bed with their stupid boyfriends. Can't you see how horrible it was this morning, to get up on my own – not a card, not a present, nothing!' Fizz pushes a large cardboard box towards me, wrapped in shiny gold paper. 'I didn't forget,' she says coldly. 'I was going to give it to you when you came home from school.'

'It's too late now. My birthday's over. I don't want anything from you, anyway.'

'Do not speak with your mother like this,' interrupts Wolfgang.

'Keep out of it! It's nothing to do with you. You're not my dad. You're not part of my family. Everything was fine until you came here!'

'Nel, there's no need to be jealous—' starts Wolfgang, but I've had enough. How dare he? I am *not* jealous! I hate him. I hate them both.

'Keep out of it!' I screech. 'Leave me alone!' I pick up my present and hurl it across the room. The box hits the stone floor with a crash of tinkling glass. For a fleeting moment I wonder what's inside – whatever it is, it's broken now. Wolfgang is staring at me as if I'm the most disgusting person that has ever walked the earth and Fizz looks as if she is about to explode. Her face has turned the same shade of purple as her hair, she's shaking all over and she's just sworn at me very badly.

'I don't care!' I shout back. 'I hate you both! I wish I'd never come here! I want to go home!'

Fizz moves towards me – I think she's going to slap my face. I flinch out of her way, and she runs past me into the kitchen. Wolfgang shoots me another filthy look and follows her, shutting the door. I can hear Fizz sobbing. Wolfgang's trying to calm her down. He's just told her that 'Nel is not worth getting upset about'. Charming. I burst into tears and run upstairs.

There, on my bed, are three envelopes – one white, one yellow and one red. I'm shaking so much I can hardly open them. The first is from Hannah – a shiny foil card with 'PARTY DUDE' written on the front. Huh! The second is from 'Dad, Julie and Alexander'. He's put a hundred pounds into my savings account so I 'can buy something I really like'. Dad has also written: 'Will ring you this evening to sing Happy Birthday.' Oh, my God! I switch on my mobile and sure enough, there are ten messages – four from Fizz and the rest from Dad, all saying things like 'Where are you? Why haven't you turned on the phone? Ring me as soon as you get my message.' And what am I going to say when he asks how his dear, sweet Eleanor celebrated her Special Day?

'Well, Dad, I woke up to no cards and no presents, had my first ever detention, wagged off school, got involved in a spot of shoplifting, fell over and twisted my ankle, saw a disgusting eighteen horror movie three times and had a massive bust up with Fizz.' Hmmm . . . I'll leave it till tomorrow. By that time I'll have made up a more believable story.

Back to my enormous pile of birthday post. One more card . . . But it isn't a card at all. It's a letter, postmarked Barcelona. It's a letter from Oriol! Yessss! At last!

Dear Nel,

I am happy because you write me the letter. I missing you. You missing me? I am at school now and it is not good. I want to be in England again. But I do not like the raining! Now juggling I am not here for school. We are coming to England next year, my father say. Very good! But I see you soon, no? I am not wait such long hours. One day I hoping you come to Barcelona. I love you, Oriol.

I love you . . . There it is in black and white (blue and white actually, but you know what I mean). Suddenly the whole horrible day melts away. What better birthday present could I have than this? Oriol still loves me! He misses me as much as I'm missing him. And he wants us to be together.

I sit on my bed and gaze out of the window at the millions of tiny stars. All at once the way forward is as clear as the night sky: I can't stay here any more, not after what happened this evening. I've got to leave as soon as I can. The penguin can have Fizz all to himself from now on. But I can't go back to Dad's because I'll only be in the way there too. I'm sick of being a nuisance, an annoying problem that nobody can get rid of. I want to be with someone who actually wants me – not because it's their turn to look after me, not because they happen to be my parent, but because they love me, for myself.

No doubt you've already guessed what I'm going to spend my birthday money on – a one-way ticket to Barcelona!

CHAPTER SEVENTEEN

It's Tuesday lunchtime and I'm in the IT room at school. We seem to have got away with our 'unauthorized absence' yesterday – at least, nobody's said anything yet. Lowenna told Mr Williams we needed the computer for a geography project – her favourite excuse for everything – and we're busy looking up Barcelona on the Internet. We can easily find information about hotels and guided walks and restaurants, but there's nothing about how to get there.

'The plane will be too expensive,' says Lowenna. 'So will the train . . . Try the coach. My Auntie Tamsin goes everywhere by coach.' So we type in 'coach travel' in the box, but all we get is a load of stuff about tours of Poland, for some bizarre reason.

'Where do the international coaches go from?' I ask Lowenna, who is now looking up the website of her favourite pop band.

'Um . . . London – London Victoria, I think . . . Yes, Victoria. We picked my auntie up from there once.'

'In that case, all I've got to do is get to Victoria. I can work out the rest when I get there.'

'I'll come with you, if you like. If you pay for my

ticket.' Lowenna and I running away to Spain together? What a hideous thought.

'That would be great, but I can't afford it. Anyway, your mum and dad will know you're missing straight away. It's easy for me. I'll just tell Fizz I'm going back to Dad's and she won't bat an eyelid.'

'Won't your dad be ringing you?'

'Yes, but on my mobile. How's he to know that I'm not on the beach in Cornwall, but in Spain!'

'You're brave,' says Lowenna admiringly. 'I don't know that I'd have the guts to do it on my own.'

'All I've got to do is get a train to London and then get on a coach! If anyone asks, don't tell them where I've gone. Promise?'

'Of course I won't! I'll miss you,' says Lowenna, with a surprising softness in her voice. 'Send us a postcard.'

So that's goodbye to Lowenna. We'll probably never see each other again. I breathe an enormous sigh of relief.

Fizz and I haven't spoken since yesterday and there hasn't been a squeak out of the penguin. The shiny gold birthday parcel has been put in the bin and they've eaten half of what looks like my birthday cake. I haven't had any, of course. I'd rather starve. Anyway, I'm too busy. I've got packing to do and a convincing lie to concoct.

'Fizz, can I have a word? In private?' (I don't trust Wolfgang not to suss me out.)

Fizz and I are standing on the clifftop, looking out at the wild green sea. I feel excited because of what I'm about to do, but also incredibly sad. This place used to be somewhere I always felt happy and at home. But now . . .

'Well?' she says coldly, after a long silence.

'I'm going back to Dad's.'

'You've spoken to him, have you?'

'Yes.'

'Oh, I see . . . When are you leaving then?'

'Tomorrow. I'll go by train, like before. I can get a bus to the station.'

'Well, if you're sure that's what you want to do,' she says, her lips pursed tightly together.

'Yes, it is.'

Fizz sighs. 'I'm not saying you have to go, but obviously I don't want to keep you here against your will.'

So that's that – all settled. No apologies, no hugs and tears – no touching mother–daughter scene that might persuade me to stay. Tomorrow morning I'll be off. How frighteningly easy it is to deceive two parents who won't talk to each other. It's their stupid fault, not mine. I'm about to jump into the black hole between Dad and Fizz and neither of them has a clue.

Less than twenty-four hours later and, believe it or not, I'm in London, at Victoria Coach Station. I stride through the doors and head for International Departures. The word 'International' makes my heart thud in my chest. I'm going to do it. I'm really going to do it. I want to skip past the rows of plastic seats, jump over the barriers and shout, 'I'm going to Barcelona!' But I've got to be calm, act grown-up. I need to find out what time the coach leaves, buy my ticket, find the right departure door . . . I can do it, I can do it.

But I need information, and not from that woman in a red suit behind the ticket desk, who looks as if she'd like to report everyone to the police. A coach is about to leave for Brussels. A small queue of people has formed and everyone is fishing around in their bags for their passports. The woman is looking bored and irritated. There is obviously a system and she expects everyone to know what it is. I'm going to study a leaflet before I make any false moves.

By a stroke of amazing luck there is a coach leaving for Barcelona at 10 p.m. It's now only four in the afternoon. Even Dad wouldn't arrive this early. Oh well, just six hours to wait. At least there's no way I can miss it! The fare is cheaper than I was expecting, so maybe I'll buy a book to read.

But now I hit a slight snag. Actually, 'slight snag' is rather a small phrase for what is in fact a *huge problem*. According to my leaflet, people under the age of fifteen cannot travel 'unaccompanied'. Eleanor Sharratt would burst into tears at this point and get on the next train home. But I remind myself that Nel Sharpe is made of stronger stuff. My heart starts thumping again, I feel my eyes pricking, but I'm not going to give in. I sit down and take out Oriol's letter. 'One day I hoping you come to Barcelona. I love you, Oriol.'

I fold up the letter and put it back in my jacket pocket. I go to the coffee bar and buy a Coke and a doughnut. Sitting at the table, I suck thoughtfully on a straw and consider altering the date of birth on my passport. But it is typed in, and covered in plastic film. Also, it is illegal. I'm going to have to show the passport to the red ogre behind the ticket desk. So what do I need to find? An adult to 'accompany' me. Easier said than done. Victoria Coach Station sends coaches all over Europe. People do not walk around wearing labels saying, 'I'm going to Barcelona!' . . . No, but their luggage does! That's it. All I have to do is wander around, spotting luggage labels. Then I choose the most likely looking person and ask them a simple favour.

So now I'm prowling around the departure lounges, casually glancing at luggage labels. I soon discover that you cannot perform such a feat casually. It involves lurking unnaturally close to people, bending my knees, leaning my head over at a strange angle and squinting. The older travellers, who have suitcases on wheels and are busy doing crosswords, obviously think I am an incredibly stupid thief. They give me a nasty glance, as if to say, 'I know what you're up to!' and tuck their cases even further in between their legs.

The younger people – who are wearing baggy clothes that they have no chance of growing into, are sprawled across several chairs. They are far easier targets. Firstly, they are asleep. Secondly, they have left their rucksacks lying all over the floor in a grand gesture of trust towards humankind. Or maybe they are just careless. Either way, it's of no help to me. I realize that not everyone is like my father, who writes the labels out a week in advance of our holidays in neat black pen. But then there is no way that Dad would ever agree to twist the regulations and accompany a fourteen-year-old runaway. All of which leads me to the conclusion that the people most likely to help me do not have labels on their luggage, so

I don't know who to ask!

I decide to buy another Coke and dream up Plan C. At least it's helping to pass the time. But there is a deadline on this, and I don't even know whether there are any seats available on this evening's coach. What if it's booked up? It's not like the number forty-seven bus. You can't stand all the way to Barcelona. Come on, Nel, I say to myself, don't panic. Eleanor couldn't do this, but you can. By tomorrow you'll be with Oriol and Los Diabolos.

I take out Oriol's letter and check the words for the seventy-seventh time. 'One day I hoping you come to Barcelona. I love you, Oriol.'

And then, as if by magic, I see the word Barcelona repeated on the front of a book. The woman on the next table is reading *Know Your Way Around Barcelona*! Which, unless fate is playing an evil trick and she is in fact travelling to Rome, means she is going there tonight! I'm about to leap over and ask the favour, when I stop. And think . . . What is the story? Let's think through the alternatives. First there is the plain, honest truth:

'Hi, I've had enough of my parents so I'm running away to join the circus.' Dad always says that it pays to tell the truth, but on this occasion I'm inclined to disagree. OK, so what about a sort of white lie . . . ?

'Hello. I'm going to visit my Spanish relations in Barcelona and my dad didn't realize that I needed to be accompanied. And he's already left because my baby brother is really ill in hospital and he had to rush back.' That's not a white lie, is it? It's a complete lie, but it sounds rather convincing! I decide to practise it a few

161

times before approaching the woman. But I daren't leave it too long. She's nearly finished her lunch and I don't want to lose her. It's now or never, Nel. Go on!

'Oh no, that's awful!' says the complete stranger. 'What's wrong with your brother?'

'He's got immature lungs.'

'The poor little thing!' The poor woman has tears in her eyes. 'Is he going to be all right?'

'We hope so. It's been very upsetting,' I reply, starting to feel rather guilty about using Alexander in this way.

'And your dad's gone all the way back to Derbyshire? Can't you ring him or something?'

'No. He'll be in the hospital all day. You can't use your mobile in hospitals.'

'Can't you? Oh dear . . . What are you going to do then?' Unfortunately, she doesn't seem to have worked out that I'm not just asking for her sympathy.

'Well, I saw you were reading that guide book. Are you going to Barcelona tonight?'

'Yes, I am! Well, I'm starting off in Barcelona, then I'm doing all of southern Spain. I know northern Spain pretty well, and I've been all over Portugal, but I've never really explored the south.'

Why is it so difficult to get through to some people? Isn't it obvious that I'm not interested in her travel itinerary? There's nothing for it but to ask outright. 'I was wondering whether you would accompany me? It's only for buying the ticket, I think. I can look after myself once we're on the coach. We don't even need to sit together.'

'Well, I don't see why not,' she muses.

'Have you bought your ticket yet? Because, if you haven't, could you buy mine at the same time? I've got the money,' I add, because she raises her eyebrows in slight suspicion at this point.

'OK,' she replies. 'I was just about to buy my ticket but there were huge queues so I thought I'd have lunch first.'

Victory!

I now have my ticket! The red ogre was simultaneously arguing with somebody on the phone so she handed it over without a second glance. Actually, Jen (that's my saviour's name) and I make a rather convincing pair. She is what is known as a Goth – which basically involves wearing a long black skirt, a black T-shirt advertising a band with an offensive name (Screaming Babies in Jen's case) and lots of spiky metal. I am in Nel mode, of course, so I can just about get away with being her younger sister or a niece. Jen's a vegetarian like Fizz and is heavily into animal rights. When I mentioned that my Spanish 'relations' were part of a circus troupe she went a little pale, but I assured her that they never worked with animals so now she's dying to meet them. She loves meeting 'people from different cultures'. She has an address book crammed with names of people she can stay with all over the world. I think she'd like to add Los Diabolos to her list. Oh well, one good turn deserves another, I suppose.

According to Jen, it will be very difficult to sleep on the coach, so she suggests we 'get some kip' now while we can. I have to say that a row of plastic chairs which go up at the sides and dig into your rib cage is not my idea of a comfortable bed. I'm so excited that I'll never sleep anyway. I can't believe that I've managed to do this. Jen is my guardian angel, sent to rescue me and guide me to Oriol. I take another peek at his letter.

'One day I hoping you come to Barcelona . . .'

I *am coming*, Oriol! And sooner than you think!

CHAPTER EIGHTEEN

We're off! The coach is crawling its way through a tangle of tatty streets, heading for the road to Dover. Jen and I have a double seat each, across the aisle from each other, so we can stretch our legs out and chat at the same time. To my surprise, there are only about twenty of us on board – let me give you a brief run-down on my fellow travellers.

At the back there is a group of middle-aged men – why do boys always want to loll about on the back seats? I heard one of them saying they were going to Lloret del Mar, which I think is a holiday resort. Then there is a couple who delight in telling everyone who will listen (and we don't have much choice) that they have a villa in Spain. If they are so well off, I wonder, why are they travelling there by coach? An elderly bloke in the row in front of me has a son who lives somewhere called Perpignan. A friendly-looking woman in a green rain-coat has a brother in Sitges. With the exception of Jen, who seems to have been round the whole world on a bus, this is our first long distance coach journey. This makes me feel anxious. Perhaps it's something most people only do once.

'What time do we arrive?' I ask Jen, who is blowing up an inflatable pillow.

'Quarter (gasp) to ten (gasp) tomorrow.'

'In the morning?'

'You must be joking! It's not a plane, you know! Quarter to ten tomorrow *evening*,' she splutters, fastening the valve. 'We've got to get all the way through France first.' Jen lies on her back with her knees in the air and rests her heavy black boots against the window. I wonder if anyone will come and tell her to put her feet down. But the two Spanish coach drivers are too busy chatting to each other, and they are probably too laid back to care anyway. She wouldn't get away with it on the school bus, that's for sure. Jen continues our conversation from this strange position, looking at the roof and speaking away from me. It's quite hard to hear what she's saying.

'So, these Spanish relations, who are they?'

'Oh, just my aunt and uncle,' I mutter.

'So, is your dad Spanish then?'

I realize I am rapidly digging a hole for myself. Some quick genealogy is required here.

'Sort of . . . They're not my immediate aunt and uncle . . . More like cousins.'

'Oh, right . . . I was going to say, you don't look Spanish . . . So, they meeting you from the coach station, then?'

'No . . .'

'Really? . . . Well, you'll have to get a taxi. Don't go on the metro late at night. It's not safe.'

'Yes, I'm going to get a taxi.' In fact, I haven't given this part of the journey a moment's thought. Now I've

166

got to make plans for getting to Oriol's apartment. I wish the coach didn't arrive so late. It's going to be quite a shock for them when I ring the doorbell – I didn't dare let him know that I was on my way, in case Fizz found out. He is going to be so surprised to see me!

'So how long you staying?' says Jen, who is now performing some strange exercise routine 'to keep her circulation moving'. Is this really necessary? We've only been on the coach for forty-five minutes.

'A fortnight.' Lie number twenty-three. I feel my cheeks reddening, and turn away to face the window. Outside it's pitch black and raining. We're on some motorway, heading into nothingness. I feel really bad about all this lying, especially when Jen is being so kind to me. 'How about you?'

'I'll stay until my money runs out. Or I might get a job. The trouble is, it's off-season, so there's not much work about.'

Jen proceeds to tell me about other places in Spain that she's visited: where there are good youth hostels, resorts to avoid, how not to spend too much in something called a tapas bar. It sounds like a lesson, and I feel I ought to be taking notes. I start to drift off, saying, 'Mmmm . . .' and 'Really?' every so often to give the impression that I'm listening. But when Jen gives me tips on the best place to change your money, I sit bolt upright and get a sudden rush of panic. I have no Spanish money on me! How can I pay for a taxi without any pesetas? Why am I such a complete idiot? Oh, well, I'll have to ask Dídac or Rosa to lend me some cash when I arrive at the apartment. I'm sure they won't mind.

We've reached Dover and have parked up in a line of coaches waiting to enter the tunnel.

'Oh, I thought we were taking the ferry!' cries Jen. 'I like the ferry. You can stretch your legs, move around. I don't like going underground. I hate those big metal boxes they put you in, they give me claustrophobia!'

I know what she means. We drive into this white container and the shutters are drawn down on either side. When we start to move it feels as if we're wobbling our way across the Channel in a giant fridge. I use my small bag as a cushion and lie down in the Jen Position. Actually, it's quite a soothing feeling, like being a baby again, rocked to sleep . . .

I'm not sure how long I slept. We've stopped somewhere and Jen is shaking me awake. 'Are we in France?' I murmur, blearily.

''Course we are! We're at a Restaurant Rapide! Come on, time for breakfast!'

One of the drivers announces that we have 'Benty minutos', which the Couple with the Villa in Spain kindly translate for us, as if we couldn't work it out for ourselves. I stumble out of the coach into the fresh morning air. It's foggy and drizzling and everywhere is grey.

'Fresh orange juice is what we need. Lots of vitamin C!' declares Jen. 'Come on, before there's a queue.'

'Nothing for me,' I mutter. 'I'm not hungry.' Lie number twenty-seven (I haven't mentioned lies twenty-four, twenty-five and twenty-six, but believe me, I told them).

'You've got to have breakfast! This'll be our only stop

till lunchtime!'

'No, I'm fine. Honestly.' (Dishonestly – I've no French money either, you understand.)

'Oh dear . . . Do you get coach-sick?'

'Yes, a bit.' At last, a grain of truth. Well, I get seasick, which is similar.

'You'd better get some fresh air then. Don't go into the café, it'll be full of smoke. French places always are.'

So Jen strides into the service station for freshly squeezed orange juice and a fat buttery croissant. And I am left to pace the car park, living out the lies that I am neither hungry nor thirsty and am about to throw up. Well, I guess it serves me right.

My tummy rumbles audibly through northern France. The drivers turn on the radio, but all the pop songs are in English, so I can hardly believe that I'm abroad. Jen sits up and complains that the scenery in this part of the country is boring. So she decides to transport me to North Africa instead, with tales of camel rides across the Sahara; oases full of date trees; tiled mosques; apple tea, souk markets and snake charmers; Berber people who live in caves; salt lakes and the Atlas mountains . . . She goes on and on and on . . . Meanwhile, I am staring out of the window at the flat green fields and scattered grubby farmhouses. I couldn't care less how boring the scenery is. I am happy to be in France. With every kilometre I am getting nearer to Oriol. I take out his letter and read it surreptitiously: 'I missing you. You missing me?'

Jen doesn't notice. She is too busy telling me how to barter in Marrakesh.

The natives are restless. We've been in the coach for nearly four hours and the boys at the back are desperate for a cigarette. 'Tourists', Jen calls them, screwing up her nose in disgust. She'd get on ever so well with Fizz. I discover that Jen is a 'Traveller'. She doesn't go sightseeing: she goes to discover other cultures, to mingle, to immerse herself. I'm not sure that there is much of a difference really, except that tourists are probably less tedious to listen to. I have started making frequent trips to the toilet just to get a few minutes' peace. It's a nasty smelling box, which doesn't seem to lock, so I'm developing the new skill of peeing with my foot against the door.

I'm afraid I sound rather negative about Jen. To be honest – and that makes a change – she is driving me crazy. Jen, as Dad would say, 'Could bore for England,' or North Africa, or the entire universe as far as I can see. But that is a terrible thing to say, and not something Nel should allow herself even to think. This woman has saved me, rescued me from the jaws of defeat and all that. But I wish to God I had spotted someone else reading *Know Your Way Around Barcelona*, because I can't take much more of her travelling tales.

The Couple with the Villa in Spain have been persuaded by Nicotine Addicts of Lloret del Mar to ask the drivers when we are going to stop for lunch, but they pretend not to understand. For some reason, they want to get this journey over as quickly as possible and pass several Restaurants Rapides, extremely rapidly before we finally draw up. I have not eaten for nineteen hours and am ready to pass out.

'Is there anywhere I can change some money?' I ask Jen, now privately re-christened the Know Your Way Around the Universe Travel Bore. How I long for a friend to be sharing this with me right now. Hannah would be perfect. She would get all my jokes and we'd spend the entire journey in hysterics of laughter.

'If you've got a cash card, you could use a hole in the wall, although they charge you commission, of course.'

I am ecstatic! I do indeed have a cash card for my savings account and to my huge relief I can even remember my secret number! I now have ten pounds worth of French francs in my hand and things are looking up. While Jen wolfs down a double portion of ratatouille and rice, I opt for chicken pieces in a delicious tomato sauce. She tells me in every gory detail about the cruelty involved in making goose pâté and how some French people even eat horse. So much for mingling with other cultures.

'I'm going to buy some more water,' announces Jen, rising from the table. 'You should drink more when travelling. It stops you getting dehydrated.'

Yeah, yeah. She walks off, looking like a large black crow. At last, I have a few moments by myself. I take out Oriol's letter and read it from the beginning: 'I am happy because you write the letter. I missing you. You missing me? I am at school and it is not good. I want to be in England again. But I do not like the raining! Now juggling I am not here for school.'

I've read that last sentence a hundred times and I still can't work out what he is trying to say! 'We are coming to England next year, my father say. Very good! But I see

171

you soon, no? I am not wait such long hours. One day I hoping you come to Barcelona. I love you, Oriol.'

'Aren't you on the Barcelona coach?' says the man with the son in Perpignan, hobbling past. 'It'll leave without us, if we don't hurry!'

I gather up my bag and jacket and we make it back to the car park as fast as we can. 'I missed a coach in the middle of the Australian outback,' boasts Jen cheerfully. I watch her let the air out of her pillow and tuck it away in her rucksack. Perhaps she sensed that I was on the verge of suffocating her with it.

'I think I'll get some sleep,' I mumble, shutting my eyes and putting my feet up on the seat. It's a shame, as the scenery has greatly improved and I rather wanted to see the Pyrenees.

Several hours have passed and I have done a superb impression of sleeping all the way through the south of France. Unfortunately, Jen decided to re-tell her stories to the woman sitting behind her so I've had to endure them all over again, although at least I didn't have to act interested. I only pretended to wake up when the coach was flagged down by the police. For a brief moment I thought they had come to get me! But no – apparently there is a problem over the drivers' schedules and they've either been driving too fast or not made enough stops. The Couple with the Villa in Spain delightedly filled us in on the full story. It turns out that the drivers are football fanatics and 'Barca' (meaning Barcelona) are playing at home tonight. Kick-off is at 9 p.m. and their aim is to get us to the city in time for them to watch the match!

We cross the Spanish border without anyone taking so much as a glimpse at our passports, so it seems they are not looking for any fourteen-year-old runaways. My mind is preoccupied with how I'm going to find a taxi. It turns out that Jen hasn't booked a hotel – I suppose it would be far too touristy. Maybe she plans to come with me to the apartment so she can do some cultural mingling with my Spanish relations. I can't face the thought of that. I'll have to sneak off as soon as the coach arrives. I decide to check the address and feel in my pocket for Oriol's letter.

A cold shiver, followed by a hot flush, rushes through my body. My heart starts to beat furiously. Where is it? I stand up and turn out my jacket pockets. I empty out my bag and examine every item. I look under my seat, I scour the corridor. I check the toilet – I even look in the little plastic bin. I don't believe it! The letter's gone! It's gone!

CHAPTER NINETEEN

'You're running away?' gasps Jen, clutching me to her chest and stroking my hair. 'Why didn't you tell me before?' I'm sobbing, rather appropriately as it turns out, all over her Screaming Babies T-shirt. But this is no time for joking observations. The situation is serious. We are just outside Barcelona and I have no idea where I am going. I must have read Oriol's letter over a hundred times, but I only studied the 'I love you' bits. Now I wish I'd memorized the address instead!

'I must have dropped the letter at the rapid restaurant place,' I mumble. 'How can I be so stupid?'

'I expect he's in the phone book,' says Jen cheerily. 'What's his surname?'

'Um, he's got two ... they're really hard to pronounce. The first one's Petosa-something? Or is it Terepo? Or Retaso – oh, now I can't remember!'

'You'll have to ring your mum, then.'

'I can't! Then she'll find out I'm in Spain!'

'Only if you tell her. Make her think you're phoning from your dad's. Tell her you want to send your boyfriend a letter and you've lost his address.'

'She'll know I'm lying ...'

'And you'd better ring your dad too, just to let him know you're safe.'

'But I'm not safe, am I?' I wail. 'I'm stranded in a foreign city with nowhere to go!'

''Course you're safe, babe, you're with me.'

'But you haven't got anywhere to stay tonight either!'

'No, but we'll find somewhere.'

'At ten o'clock at night?'

'Of course! The Spanish aren't like us boring old English, you know, tucked up in bed with a cup of cocoa. They don't even eat their evening meal till ten!'

The coach enters what is obviously the city centre – wide streets lined with pale elegant buildings. The other passengers are getting their bags together and pointing out of the window with excitement. I never thought I'd say this, but right now I'd rather be in Derby.

'Don't worry about it now. We'll work something out in the morning,' says Jen calmly. 'Ooh, look at that amazing building! It's all patterned and curvy!'

The coach draws up by the main railway station. Most of the passengers are being met by delighted relations who hug them and swoop up their suitcases, hurrying them off to a waiting car, a meal and a comfortable bed, no doubt. I've never felt so jealous of complete strangers. Here am I, completely dependent on a woman I earlier wanted to suffocate. I have nearly forgotten all her boring stories, and I have certainly forgiven her for them. She is my guardian angel again, and my soul is in her hands. Her obsession with wearing black and her passion for loud grunge music makes her an unlikely candidate for the job, but she's all I've got right now, and I'm not in a position to be choosy. My guardian angel fishes out *Know Your Way Around Barcelona* and decides that we should catch the metro to the Barrio Gótic. Apparently this is where the cheapest accommodation can be found.

'I thought it wasn't safe to catch the metro at night,' I mutter as we struggle through the ticket barriers with our luggage.

'It's not,' Jen replies cheerfully, 'but it's cheaper than a taxi, and you need to save money.'

I sit on the train with my bags on my lap, clasped to me as if they contain the crown jewels. Nobody seems in the least bit interested in stealing them, but then maybe that's part of the trick. Maybe the person I should be most suspicious of is that old lady in the corner, falling asleep in between stops. We emerge from the metro station and it's time to consult the map again.

'That's the cathedral over there by the look of it,' says Jen. 'So, we want to go *this* way.'

We make our way up a pedestrianized street, which narrows with every step. There are no street lamps, just gloomy lights from shop windows and restaurants. Suddenly the street opens out into a large cobbled square, full of people. A punk band is playing, someone is shouting through the microphone, and there is a banner strewn across a raised wooden stage. Armed police in shirtsleeves are standing round the edges of the crowd, managing to look bored and threatening at the same time, which is no mean feat.

'Looks like some sort of anarchist protest,' says Jen, her eyes lighting up. 'I wonder what it's about.' She puts her bag on the ground and looks expectantly at the stage, as if she's suddenly going to be able to understand Catalan.

'Hadn't we better find a hotel first?' I suggest.

'S'pose so . . . Perhaps we'll come back later.'

I hope not. All this stress is exhausting me. The thought of being tucked up in bed with a cup of English cocoa is starting to sound very appealing. We leave the anarchists and make our way towards the first place on Jen's list. I try to stop at a bright hotel with large, inviting windows, but Jen drags me away from the door.

'Forget it! It's got three stars!' We can't afford to stay in a proper hotel. We've got to find a *hostal*.'

'What's that, like a youth hostel?'

'Sort of . . .' she replies vaguely. It's starting to sound ominous.

But why should I be worried? When I'm with Fizz we never use hotels. If we can't find friends to stay with, we camp or sleep in Daisy. It's only Eleanor who stays in hotels – large modern blocks in Tenerife, with hundreds of balconies and swimming pools and a kids 'mini disco' every night. Eleanor likes hotels with air-conditioning and luxurious bathrooms and a tiny fridge. Whereas Nel hates package holidays. She's the adventuress, who spurns planning and organization. She just packs her bags and sets off without a care in the world . . . Hmm . . . Right at this moment, I think Eleanor has a lot more sense.

Thinking of Dad and Fizz is helping to distract me from the growing realization that Jen and I have just entered the set of a black-and-white horror film. The Barrio Gótic is a maze of gloomy alleyways, flanked with tall, grey, dirty buildings. I've just tripped over a drunk lying in the doorway of some old church. Above us is a row of stone gargoyles, whose hideous heads are throwing huge shadows across the pavement. In another doorway a busker with a nasty sense of humour is playing ghostly flute music. If he thinks I'm going to throw him a peseta he must be completely mad. All we need now is for a vampire to swoop down and offer us a room for the night in Hostal Dracula. It could be the only offer we get. We have tried five *hostals* so far and every one has been 'completo' – loosely translated as 'fully booked by sensible people who make their accommodation arrangements in advance'.

'Let's try down here,' says Jen, who is sounding a lot less chirpy than she was half an hour ago. It's too dark to read the map, so now we are just wandering around in circles (or should I say squares). 'As long as we don't stray into the Barrio Chino,' she mutters, 'we'll be OK.'

So there's somewhere worse than this?

'What will we do if we can't find anywhere?' I ask. The strap on my bag is digging into my shoulder, I'm sweating in my thick jacket and my fingers are clasped so tightly around the top of my handbag that they're turning numb. I might as well wear a big sticker on my forehead saying, '*Hola!* I'm a stupid tourist, please mug me!'

'Let's try that place.' Jen points to a large neon sign, which says PENSION. The only pension that I know is collected by old people at the post office, but Jen assures me that this is another name for a *hostal*. We open a large wooden door and climb two flights of stairs until we reach an incredibly gloomy lobby, lit only by a small television set showing the final moments of the Barcelona football match. The old man at the desk studiously ignores us, as he waits to see if his team has beaten Leeds United. I don't wish to be unpatriotic, but I'm hoping Barcelona win. If they don't, he may refuse English travellers a room out of spite. But luckily for us, Barca secures a 2–1 victory. The old man raises a fist and shouts at the television.

Meanwhile, Jen is squinting at the 'Useful Spanish Phrases' section of her guide book. 'I wish he'd switch the light on,' she mutters, clearing her throat and leaning across the counter.

The man is now absorbed in the after-match chat, but we can't afford to wait. If this place is *completo* too, we need to move on. Now I know what Mary and Joseph must have felt like when they arrived in Bethlehem, to be told there was 'no room at the inn'. If I ever get to perform in another Nativity play, which seems unlikely, I will know exactly how to play the part.

'*Una habi-tac-ión para dos per-sonas,*' says Jen.

'*Por favor,*' I add. I'm so well trained by Dad that I have to say 'please' and 'thank you', even in a crisis. Especially in a crisis, actually.

'*Si . . .*' he replies, without taking his eyes from the screen.

My heart leaps with relief, gratitude, joy. I want to run round the lobby with my top over my head like the footballer they've just been showing on the replays. Victory for the English at last.

It's the adverts now, so he turns to face us and demands to see our passports. Then he writes '3,500' on a scrap of paper.

179

'But I haven't got any Spanish money!' I gasp.

'Don't worry, I have,' says Jen, unzipping her bag. 'You can pay me your share tomorrow once you've changed your money.'

'How much is it?'

'Oh, about fourteen quid. Not bad for the two of us.'

It seems incredibly cheap to me, and I start to wonder what exactly we're going to get for the money: a pile of straw in the corner of the stable? We are given an enormous key and some instructions that seem to involve climbing more stairs, if the man's gestures are anything to go by. If I weren't so worn out, I'd run up every one.

I never thought I'd be so pleased to be sleeping on a lumpy mattress in threadbare nylon streets! Actually, I can't sleep. It's far too noisy out there, even though it's two o'clock in the morning. The cathedral bells chime every quarter of an hour, drunken football fans are roaming the streets singing at the tops of their voices (rather tunefully, in fact, so they can't be English) and somebody seems to be fixing their motorbike outside our window. Jen is in the other bed, snoring blissfully. There is no plug in the sink, no soap, no towel. She said we were lucky to have running water at all, but told me not to drink it.

I'm dying of thirst, and wonder whether she'd mind if I drank some of the mineral water in the bottle lying temptingly at her side. I'd also like to go to the loo, but the bathroom is down the end of the corridor and I'm too scared to leave the room. I've only been here a few hours and I've already got enough news to write a dozen postcards to Hannah. She will be so-ooo impressed! Of course, I won't mention the floods of tears and panic attacks. On second thoughts, parents can read postcards, and even an envelope with a Spanish stamp is going to rouse suspicion. I don't want Hannah's mum leaping to the telephone to alert Dad. No, I've got to keep under-cover, at least until I've found Oriol.

The big problem is how?

CHAPTER TWENTY

Jen and I have spent a fruitless morning asking people if they know where Los Diabolos live. Nobody seems to have a clue what we're talking about, and Jen's 'Useful Spanish Phrases' section hasn't helped us much. We can ask, 'Dónde está la catedral?' and 'Dónde está la banco?' with confidence, but 'Dónde está Los Diabolos?' has been greeted with raised eyebrows and vigorous shakes of the head. A friendly guide in the tourist office has just explained that we've actually been asking people, 'Where is the devils?' Jen's flowing black skirt, dyed black hair and deathly pale skin can only have added to the impression that we were two witches searching for a bit of Spanish black magic!

'Diabolos . . . of course, like diabolical! Of the devil!' exclaims Jen as we walk wearily past the cathedral for the fourth time.

'Is that what diabolical means? I thought it meant really awful.'

'Don't be daft. Who'd call their circus company the Awful Ones?' she giggles.

I don't know how she can be so cheerful. We've been on our feet all morning, trudging in and out of alternative-looking shops, tourist offices and cafés. I'm exhausted. Now we're back in the Barrio Gótic, which we've discovered means the Gothic Quarter. Being a confirmed Goth herself, Jen is feeling very much at home in this jumble of medieval buildings and Roman walls.

I have to admit it's not at all scary in the daylight. The place is full of tourists wandering around taking photos of each other in front of fountains, elderly couples are painting insipid watercolours, and I'm saying, 'This place is awesome,' instead of 'This is giving me the creeps.'

We turn a corner and suddenly find ourselves in a large, attractive square, decked with palm trees and elaborate lampposts. The sun is shining and the sky is a bright cloudless blue. It's so warm I can hardly believe it's October. I collapse on a chair outside a café, while Jen studies the menu to see if we can afford to eat in such elegant surroundings. We can't, but I refuse to go another step. So she orders the cheapest thing on the menu – two cheese rolls and a glass of water.

'I want to walk up the Ramblas this afternoon,' Jen announces, crumbs of bread sticking to her dark purple lipstick. 'According to the book, it's *the* place to go.'

But I don't want to sightsee. I want to find Oriol. 'It's ridiculous,' I sigh. 'What am I going to do?'

'You've got to phone your mum!' insists Jen. 'There's no other way.'

'But I'm scared!'

'You'll be fine, as long as you play it dead casual . . .'

'OK . . .' I take out my mobile and dial. My fingers are trembling. But the phone won't connect – I must have dialled wrong. I try again, but still nothing happens.

'I think it has to be "dual band" to work abroad,' says Jen. 'Is it a cheap one?'

'The cheapest Dad could get hold of,' I reply miserably. 'I suppose I could use a phone box instead . . .'

'Looks like you'll have to.'

'But what if Fizz says she'll ring me back with the address? She's bound not to have it on her. Or what if my money runs out while she's trying to find it? What if . . . what if—?'

'Let's face it,' Jen interrupts, 'she's going to find out soon enough. Phone her now and tell her the truth.'

I'm starting to realize that Jen has had enough of the guardian angel job and wants to move on. I don't blame her. It can't be much fun wandering around with a stranded teenager asking people peculiar questions. She wants to go to the Picasso Museum, to do what she calls the Modernist Trail. She wants to walk round the market and show off her bartering skills. I'm just a nuisance, soon to be immortalized as 'the time I met this stupid fourteen-year-old girl who was running away to the circus'. I'm not her friend. I'm just a story for her next long-distance coach trip.

I work out the code for dialling England and take the plunge. My hand is shaking as I hold the receiver to my ear. The phone rings . . . and rings . . . and rings . . . I don't understand it. Fizz always puts the answerphone on when she goes out, in case someone wants to book her act. She must be there! The pattern of bleeps – two short ones, then a gap, then two short ones – forms a rhythm in my head. Bleep, bleep . . . bleep, bleep . . . bleep,

bleep . . . Is she on the loo? Asleep? Come on, Fizz, answer the phone!! Bleep, bleep . . . bleep, bleep . . .

'No reply,' I announce glumly.

'Try again later.' Jen picks up her rucksack. 'Come on, let's walk up the Ramblas.'

The Ramblas turns out to be a long, wide street with a pedestrianized area in the middle. Sorry, Jen has just corrected me. It's actually five wide streets, one after the other. Jen is so busy studying the guide book that she's not actually looking at anything and has just walked into a newspaper stand, which I have to say I found rather funny, although I managed not to laugh out loud. I think I'll give my own description rather than the one provided in *Know Your Way Around Barcelona*. I'll start again.

The Ramblas turn out to be five long, wide streets with a pedestrianized area in the middle. There are several hotels; gift shops; stylish bakeries selling tempting but expensive cakes; tiny museums you hardly notice; pizza places; trendy bars and pavement cafés on either side. The central area is littered with colourful stalls, which change as you pass unwittingly from *rambla* to *rambla*. The flower stalls spill onto the pavement – tubs of lilies, orchids, roses and other exotic-looking plants with impossible names. A man with greasy hair in a shiny grey suit is having his shoes cleaned, and a small group has gathered round somebody performing card tricks. It's a place for browsing, stopping and staring, for soaking up the atmosphere – and having your wallet pinched, if you're not careful.

But I find it impossible to think of any of these dark-haired, olive-skinned people as thieves and pickpockets. Everyone is a potential Oriol. A particular walk, the back of a head, the colour of a shirt . . . My eyes become fixed on a young man striding ahead. Could it be? Could it? My heart starts to pound and I quicken my pace. Then, just as I'm about to shout his name, he turns round and reveals an unfamiliar face. I catch myself staring and quickly look in the other direction. And straight away there's another one, in jeans this time, with just the same kind of trainers. But he's holding hands with a girl. It can't be Oriol, can it? I need to check his face just to make sure it's not him, but Jen is dragging me across the road to see some 'incredible' shop façade she's just spotted. The boy I hope isn't Oriol merges into the crowd. What if that was him? It's a new form of teenage torture.

We have just stepped into the Boqueria – a large covered market which looks as if it's taken over a Victorian railway station. Jen pulls me past an amazing mix of brightly coloured fruit and vegetables, long garlicky sausages, huge bunches of dried red chilli peppers and marble slabs covered with exotic looking fish. 'My God,' she cries in horror, as we pass a bowl of squirming eels. 'They're still alive!' As a vegetarian, I thought she'd be pleased.

But I'm not interested in the region's agricultural produce, all I'm looking at is faces. The young lad wheeling a trolley of lemons has Oriol's large brown eyes, the woman serving up saucers of squid at the stand-up snack bar has his dark wavy hair and the man leaning against the counter has the same thin, straight nose. But recognizing random features is not enough. I want to be able to see them in one person. I want to see Oriol! Scanning the horde of faces is making me feel dizzy. I can't see for looking, as Dad says. I never really knew what that phrase meant until now.

Jen buys two huge oranges and leads me back onto the street. 'Let's find somewhere to sit down,' she suggests. We park ourselves on a couple of wooden chairs that are screwed into the pavement. A woman wearing a jingling jester's hat, velvet knickerbockers and yellow tights whizzes past us on a unicycle.

'She'll know where Los Diabolos live!' I shout, with my mouth full of pips. But the medieval jester wobbles round the corner and vanishes before I even have a chance to stand up. I start to wonder if I imagined her, like a desperate traveller seeing a mirage in the desert.

'You could try asking some of the statues,' says Jen, licking the juice from her fingers.

This remark is not as stupid as it sounds. All along the Ramblas are young men covered in body make-up, wearing outlandish costumes, all standing completely still in various strange poses. For some reason this is meant to be entertaining. I can't see the point of it myself. I presume they are only doing this because they are not capable of juggling or performing acrobatics. But the tourists seem to like them. Each statue attracts its own crowd of photo snappers, who throw a few pesetas into a box before moving on to the Green Alien, or the silver St George, or the overgrown Angel Gabriel, white from head to toe with huge feathery wings. I suppose I could go up to one and ask, 'Where is the devils?' but I'm pretty sure I wouldn't get a response. As a rule, even human statues don't talk.

'There's another phone booth,' remarks Jen, over-casually. 'Fizz might be home now.'

I dial the number again. The familiar sequence of bleeps invades my head. Yet I can't put the phone down. An old man is looking at me rather impatiently: it's obvious to him that the person I'm calling is out. But I keep thinking, Maybe Fizz is rushing in from the beach, maybe she and the penguin are having yet another bath or she's got loud music on and has only just heard the phone. She's probably just about to pick up the receiver . . . I'll give her one more ring – No, two . . . four . . . ten . . .

'Any luck?' Jen asks.

I shake my head. We pick up our bags and move further up the Ramblas. We reach what, according to my friendly guide, is known locally as the Rambla dels Ocells, which basically means that the flower stalls have been replaced by caged birds. I have to agree with Jen that none of the little creatures looks very happy and you couldn't say any of them have been overfed.

'It's disgusting,' she cries. 'Why isn't anybody protesting about it?'

I do hope she's not about to commit an act of animal rights terrorism and release the birds into the skies. I feel I've got enough to worry about at the moment, without the fate of a few bored budgerigars. 'Perhaps Fizz's gone away,' I murmur. 'She might have gone to Germany.'

'How would *they* like to be stuck in a cage all day!' Jen continues, obviously far more concerned about the birds than about me. 'I bet nobody even buys them.

They're probably only here so the stupid tourists can take photos.'

'What am I going to do?' I say to Barcelona in general, gazing at the anonymous passers-by. My eyes fix on a human statue, a young man with thin legs covered in gold body paint. He is wearing black knee-breeches, a black embroidered waistcoat, and is waving a red cloak like a bullfighter. I expect Jen will have something to say about *him* next – no doubt he's encouraging cruelty to animals. I edge a little closer. Two dark eyes peep out of his gold face. On his head is a triangular cap with green braid. He makes me want to laugh. I see him blink a few times, then he starts to wobble. There is a sigh of disappointment from the small crowd.

'Nel!' the statue cries, suddenly coming to life. It springs off its wooden plinth and runs over to me. 'Nel!' The red bullfighter grips my shoulders and plants a kiss on either of my cheeks. I'm staring at him, speechless with shock. Is this real? Please don't let this be another mirage! Please!

'Oriol!' I finally gasp. 'Is it really you?' Of course it's really him. Who else is it going to be? Come on, Nel, get a grip!

'Nel, you here! It's fantasteek! You don't say you here. Why you here? Where is Fizz?'

I'm too happy and relieved to answer any questions. Gold make-up has come off on my T-shirt – on my arms, on my face too, no doubt – but I couldn't care less.

Jen wanders up, holding a terrified blue budgie in a tiny cage. 'You've found him!' I nod furiously, grabbing Oriol's arm to make sure he doesn't get away. 'Aren't you going to introduce us, then?' she grins.

Oriol abandons his statue existence, and leads us to a tiny bar down a side street, where he gallantly buys us all a glass of Coke. I try to tell Oriol as simply and as slowly as possible that I have come to Barcelona to be with him. I really wish Jen would leave us alone. This is meant to be a deeply romantic moment! She is dividing her attentions between us and her new feathered friend, whom she's christened Carlos. I imagine she's only bought Carlos so that she can release him into the wild. As I believe budgerigars come from Australia, the poor thing is obviously a long way from home. So maybe they'd like to start the journey *now*. But no, she's quite happy here, with me and Oriol. Thanks a lot, Jen.

'I no understand,' says Oriol, stroking my hand as he speaks. I know this sounds ridiculous, but it's actually sending shivers up and down my spine! 'You here, always?'

'That's right. I've come on my own. To be with you.'

'I no understand. Where is Fizz?'

'In Cornwall . . . I think. Or Germany. She and Wolfgang have fallen madly in love. You remember Wolfgang. The penguin?'

'Your mum is in love with a penguin?' interrupts Jen, obviously thinking Fizz is a fellow bird enthusiast.

I let out a long, weary sigh. If I can't even make myself understood to an English person, I've got no chance with Oriol. 'He's a German saxophonist. He just dresses up as a penguin,' I explain irritably.

'Whatever for?'

'To earn money. Look, it doesn't matter.'

Throughout this pointless exchange Oriol has been staring thoughtfully at the ice melting at the bottom of his glass. Either he's completely confused or he wants to say something but doesn't know the English words. I suspect it's a bit of both.

'I'm so glad to see you,' I say, leaning across the table and kissing his smudged gold cheek.

'We go to my apartment,' he says finally, with a serious look on his face. 'We talk with my parents.' Yes, I know it sounds ominous, but he means Rosa and Dídac, so it'll be fine . . . Won't it?

'Good idea!' says Jen as if the 'we' included all of us. 'Let's go back to the *hostal* and get the rest of our luggage.'

It's not quite the romantic reunion I'd imagined. I'd pictured the two of us walking hand in hand along the beach. The sun would be setting in a warm orange glow, the Mediterranean lapping at our feet. Oriol would turn to me and say in his sexy Spanish accent, 'I haf love for you.' And then he'd kiss me . . .

Instead Oriol, still dressed as a bullfighter, has just pushed me onto a crowded bus, accompanied by a gothic witch and a screeching budgerigar. No amount of imaginings could have come up with that bizarre picture, I can tell you. But I mustn't complain. By some miracle, in a city of a million people (no, *three* million people, Jen informs me), I have found him!

CHAPTER TWENTY-ONE

'You came on your owns?' gasps Rosa. 'Fizz does not know you are here?'

'No . . . We had a big argument – A row,' I try to explain.

Rosa translates for Dídac who shakes his head in disbelief. 'Nel! This is a bad thing! The city is not good for girls, you understand?'

'I know. But I had to come. I wanted to be with Oriol, with all of you.'

'But, Nel, you came on your owns!'

'Actually, she came with me,' interrupts Jen, who has spent the last few minutes sitting quietly in the corner, feeding crisps to Carlos.

'Jen travelled with me on the coach. She's been looking after me.'

'You are lucky, very lucky, Nel – you are . . .' Rosa is so exasperated she has to finish her sentence in Catalan. She and Dídac exchange a few words, Oriol joins in and is told to keep out of it – at least that's what it sounds like from the tone of Dídac's voice. Rosa rummages through a drawer for her address book and disappears into the hallway. I presume she's phoning Fizz. Help!

I'm feeling rather guilty and very stupid. Rosa and Dídac are parents after all, and are reacting with that traditional grown-up mixture of shock, anger and disappointment. At least Oriol keeps smiling and winking at me, as if to say, 'Don't worry, everything's going to be all right.' But is it? Rosa is talking with Fizz half in English, half in Spanish. I'm trying to eavesdrop on the English bits, but that stupid budgie is chirping at the top of his tiny voice so I can't make out what they're saying. After a few minutes Rosa calls me to the phone. Oh dear.

'Best of luck,' murmurs Jen.

'Thanks. I'm going to need it.'

'Nel! You must be mad! What made you think you could just go to Spain and join somebody else's family? You're fourteen, for God's sake!'

'Well, nobody else wanted me.'

'Oh, don't be so ridiculous! We've had the police searching for you for the past twenty-four hours.'

'What?' A cold shiver runs right through me. 'How come?'

'Colin's been trying and trying to get you on your mobile. In the end he rang the cottage and I told him you'd caught the train to Derby on Wednesday morning. We thought you'd been abducted, murdered . . . They were about to print your photo in the national newspapers! I haven't slept.'

'Oh, I'm sorry.'

'Sorry? You've no idea what we've been through!' Fizz adds some other choice phrases about what I've just done that I don't feel inclined to repeat. Basically, I only did it to get attention, I've wasted the police's time, I'm nothing but trouble and it's a miracle I'm not dead. In other words, she's not very pleased with me.

'I'm sorry, Fizz, really I am.'

'You'd better ring your father straight away. He's at home. I'll call the police and tell them you're safe.'

Oh, God. If that's the reception I get from Fizz, what is Dad going to say? I'm about to find out.

'Eleanor! Oh, my God, it's Eleanor!' I can just make out somebody shrieking in the background, I haven't a clue who. 'Where are you? Are you all right? What happened? We thought, we thought . . . Where are you?'

'In Spain. Barcelona.'

Stunned silence from Dad. 'Barcelona?'

'Yes . . . I ran away to be with my boyfriend.'

'But . . . but, you haven't got a boyfriend.'

'I have, Dad. He's a circus performer. I'm here with his family.'

'His family knew about this?'

'No, no . . . Nor did he. I did it all by myself.'

'But why, Eleanor, why?'

Long silence.

'I didn't think you or Fizz wanted me.'

'Oh, Eleanor . . .' Dad heaves an enormous sigh. 'Look, I'll be over on the next plane. Give me an address.'

Weird . . . I thought the Big Telling Off would come from Dad, but it didn't. He was just really happy to hear my voice. In fact, he started crying. When the phone call was over, Fizz rang again and spoke to Rosa. Apparently, she's coming over on the next plane too. Yikes! How am I going to manage with both of them? I can see myself

194

rushing from room to room as if I'm acting in some sit-com, one minute Eleanor, the next, Nel. Are they both going to insist on taking me back? Is there going to be a 'tug of love' battle? A fight even? A duel on the beach at dawn?

Rosa tells Jen, very kindly, that there isn't room for her to stay in their tiny apartment, especially now 'more visitors' are on their way. Everyone thanks her for looking after me so well, and keeping me safe and Jen insists on taking their address so that she can 'keep in touch'.

'Thanks, Jen,' I say. 'I couldn't have done it without you.'

'Your problems aren't over yet,' she grins. 'Good luck. Maybe I'll see you again. You never know!'

'Have a good time! *Adios!*'

'Yeah . . . *Adios!*'

So, that's Jen (and Carlos) fading out of my life. In the end I was quite fond of the Know Your Way Around the Universe Travel Bore. All the same, I think I'll avoid travelling by coach in future – just to be safe.

I spent a rather awkward evening with Los Diabolos (well, Dídac, Rosa and Oriol, Jordi lives elsewhere with his family and works nights as a car mechanic). Rosa seems cross with Oriol. I don't think she believes that he wasn't part of the plan. I've told her several times that he had nothing to do with it, but she's convinced that I'm protecting him. Poor Oriol. Now he's in trouble too, and it's all my fault.

Would you believe it, Dad and Fizz are arriving on the *same plane*, which gets in from Heathrow this afternoon!

I hope for everyone's sake they aren't sitting next to each other. Dídac is going to meet them at the airport. I feel terrible about all the trouble I'm putting them too. I just want to hide! I don't want to be Nel or Eleanor. I want to be Nobody, Miss Invisible, Miss Never Existed. I can't confide in Oriol, because he doesn't understand English well enough. He's trying his best to comfort me (whilst watching football on television), but Rosa won't let us be on our own together.

She's very suspicious of us – she must think we're going to make plans to run away. I wish! I wonder if Oriol would come with me. Maybe we could go to South America. That's where people go when they want to vanish, isn't it? They speak Spanish over there too. I'm starting to fantasize how we'd do it, whether there's enough money left in my savings account to buy a ticket. If not, perhaps we could stow away on a boat. It would be so romantic . . . and impossible. Forget it, Nel, you've been caught and nobody's going to let you out of their sight again. I'm a virtual prisoner. Rosa isn't going to let me out of the apartment until Dad and Fizz get here.

Isn't it strange? For years I've longed for my parents to be together – not as husband and wife again (I'm not that idealistic) but to talk to each other, to be friendly. Now they're on their way, I'm wishing they were a world apart. What on earth am I going to say to them?

'Darling!' Fizz runs over and gives me a suffocating cuddle, as if it's the first round in the Which Parent Hugs the Hardest competition.

'Eleanor!' cries Dad. 'I'm so glad you're safe!'

'I'm so sorry, so sorry,' I gasp, when I finally come up for air. 'You didn't have to come. I could have gone back by myself.'

'Don't be silly. Of course we had to come.'

'You've got nothing to apologize for. It's all our fault.'

'Yes . . . Colin's right. We've let you down, Nel. I'm really sorry.'

Wait a minute! Let's freeze the frame here – did I just imagine that conversation or did they just *agree* about something? And even more freaky, did they really just use the words 'our' and 'we'? I look from one to the other. They've been talking, haven't they? They've had a discussion about this! My God! My parents have had a conversation, their first in about nine years!

'If we had been grown-up enough to communicate with each other, this never would have happened,' explains Dad – in a rather formal way, as if he's been rehearsing it. But it doesn't matter. It's amazing to hear, however he says it.

'We didn't realize what you were going through,' adds Fizz. They sit on either side of me on the sofa. 'Poor Nel.'

'Tell us what's been going on,' says Dad.

Oh dear. It's time for the Moment of Truth.

Long silence . . . I don't know what to say! Everything I'm feeling sounds so stupid when I say it out loud. They're both staring at me with this 'I'm really listening' look on their faces, and it's putting me off. Can I tell them what I'm really thinking at the moment? How do you say, 'I don't know who I am,' without sounding like a complete nutter who should be carted off to the loony bin? But it's true. *I don't know who I am.* Maybe it's because I've got them both here together, so it doesn't feel right being either Nel or Eleanor. But maybe I've never been just Nel or Eleanor – maybe I've always been a third person, an uncomfortable mixture of both. There's more to it than clothes and a hairstyle, more to it than changing my name every few weeks. It's about how I feel inside. But, if I'm neither Nel nor Eleanor, who the hell am I?

'Talk to us, Eleanor,' prods Dad gently.

'Please, Nel. We want to know.'

OK, let's do it. Let's *do it*. 'You said it just now. You know me as Eleanor, Dad. And Fizz thinks of me as Nel. I have to be two different people.'

'And who would you rather be?' asks Fizz slowly.

I suppose she wants me to answer Nel, and Dad wants me to answer Eleanor. I can feel them tugging at me, ever so gently. Perhaps that's why I'm so tall and long – they've been stretching me between them for years.

'I don't know. I don't think I'm Nel or Eleanor, really. I'm someone else, someone in between. Someone nobody knows . . . Oh, I can't explain. It sounds silly.'

'Try,' urges Dad. 'We want to hear.'

'When I'm Eleanor, everything's normal and organized . . . and boring, really. But I know it's got to be boring because I have to go to school and things. There's more freedom when I'm Nel, it's more fun. I thought I wanted to be Nel all the time – that's why I went back to Cornwall . . .'

'So, why didn't it work out?' says Dad, after a long silence.

This is very tricky. I can't really explain without

making Fizz look bad. They know why I'm hesitating, looking at the floor, suddenly finding an intense interest in the beads round my wrist.

'I suppose I'm not used to being a mum,' sighs Fizz. 'I didn't really do what you expected, did I? You wanted me to be more like your dad.'

'I don't know, Fizz. I don't know what I want.' I've got to do better than this, otherwise we won't get anywhere. Let's try again: 'When I'm Nel, I'm different. Most of the time, that's really good. But the trouble with Nel is that she does . . . stupid things. She doesn't think things through. And she doesn't choose very good friends, either. There was this girl . . .'

'And?'

'I got into some trouble in Northquay. When you called the police, they didn't say anything, did they?'

'About what?'

'Oh, nothing . . .'

'*What?*' they repeat in unison. Me and my big mouth.

'Nothing . . . Just this girl I made friends with, she took some stuff from a shop, and I sort of helped . . . I didn't mean to do it. I was just angry.'

'Oh, Eleanor,' sighs Dad painfully.

Fizz turns and looks me straight in the eyes. 'What was making you angry, Nel?'

'I don't know . . .' Long pause. More bracelet-fiddling. I discover that the rug has a fascinating geometric pattern. Of course, I know what was making me angry. But am I going to tell them? This is turning into one of those heavy parental 'talks' that seem never to end. They go on for so long that you feel your eighteenth birthday's going to come and go during one of the silences and you'll grow up without realizing it. There are only two ways to make these agonizing sessions come to an end. Either you tell them what's really on your mind, or you burst into tears and storm out of the room. The trouble with the second option is that they come and find you and it starts all over again. I can't bear it.

'*You* were making me angry. You and Dad.'

'Why?'

'I don't fit in anywhere any more. On one side it's you, Julie and the baby, Dad. On the other it's you and Wolfgang, Fizz. I suppose I'm jealous – because you love them more than me . . . ' Oh! I didn't expect that to come out! Is that what I really feel? Am I just jealous? God, that's a bit pathetic, isn't it? Yes . . . pathetic, but sadly true.

'I don't love Julie more than you,' insists Dad. 'It's not the same. It's a completely different kind of love.'

'Absolutely,' agrees Fizz. 'You can't compare them.' Yes, well, I don't really want to go into all that.

'I'm not jealous of Alexander, though,' I insist, which is true. Definitely true. 'I love Alexander. I always wanted a brother or sister and now I've got one. Well, half of one . . . I know I'll never have a proper one, but I'm pleased he's here. Really I am. How is he, by the way? Is he OK?'

'Yes, he's doing really well. Go on.'

'There's not much more to say. We had that big bust-up on my birthday and I thought, The only people I really want to be with are Los Diabolos. And Oriol. I just wanted to be with Oriol.'

'So you ran away to the circus,' says Dad, stroking my hair. 'Oh dear, you poor thing. What are we going to do with you?'

Well, I think, you could leave me here with Oriol and Los Diabolos, but I don't bother to reply. Because it's not going to happen, is it? I realize now that it was just one of Nel's romantic ideas. Running away to the circus – it sounds so ridiculous when you put it like that. No, I'll be back on the plane with them tomorrow, no doubt, back to my life of to-ing and fro-ing, up and down the motorway, school days and holidays, alternating Christmases . . . Nothing will change.

But hang on! I shouldn't be so pessimistic. It may have been a stupid idea to run away to Barcelona, but it's finally brought them face to face, hasn't it? At least they're talking to each other now. There's no need to go back to hiding in the service station and refusing to speak on the phone. Didn't Dad admit that they should have communicated with each other? This is a moment I should grab, because it might never come again.

'What I really hate,' I venture slowly, 'is the fact that you never talk to each other. I know you don't like each other any more, but you *must* have once. Or I wouldn't have been born. You must even have *loved* each other once.' Uh-oh, I've just moved into some rather dangerous territory.

'Yes, Nel,' nods Fizz, 'we did love each other – a lot. The day you were born was the happiest day of my life.'

'Mine too,' says Dad. 'But we were too different. We loved each other, but somehow being together just didn't make us happy. When we were together, we didn't feel that we were being ourselves. Does that make sense?'

'Of course it does. It's how I feel when I'm with you. Either of you,' I add, in case Fizz thinks it doesn't apply to her.

She squeezes my hand. 'I loved you so much, Nel, but I just had to go away and do my own thing.'

'And I never forgave you for it,' mumbles Dad.

'I don't blame you, Colin. I only went because I knew you'd take better care of her than me.'

My God! Now they can't *stop* talking to each other. Aren't parents the weirdest people? I'm sitting in the middle of them, turning my head from side to side as if I'm watching a tennis match. Out it all comes . . . They're both crying now, and it's my turn to comfort them and calm them down.

'The good thing is that you're talking now,' I say. 'I can't tell you how great it is, just to have the two of you in the same room. It makes me feel . . . well, it's hard to describe. It's like I'm one whole person at last.'

It *does* feel like that, you know. I'm not sure who this single person is yet. I don't know what name I'm going to give her either – Nel, Eleanor: suddenly neither of them seems right. But I can't talk any more – I'm exhausted. God knows what Los Diabolos are making of all this, relegated to the kitchen while we three sob and embrace in a very un-English way. All this crying can't be doing anything for my appearance. Thank God I put on my waterproof mascara this morning. I hope Oriol doesn't decide I'm an ugly, emotional wreck!

Do you know what I think? Maybe we *never* know who we are. Or maybe we know who we are all the time. Because it might be far simpler than we try to make it. We are who we are, and it's not a fixed thing. We change from moment to moment, breath to breath. That's how it is, and how it should be . . . Sorry. That didn't make any sense, did it? I'm too tired and it's been a very long day.

It's late evening and we've just finished dinner at this lovely restaurant on the sea front. It's been very strange to see Dad and Fizz sitting around the same table together, with Dídac and Rosa, Oriol and me. Anyone passing by might have taken us for three couples. I wish Jordi had been there too. He never says much, but it just doesn't feel right without him. Dídac and Dad both chose the steak – it really made me laugh!

The grown-ups are drinking coffee and some Spanish liqueur Dídac insisted on ordering, so Oriol and I took the chance to escape. We've only got another day before the three of us fly back to England, but at least Dad and Fizz have agreed that I can come out to see Oriol at Christmas. I can hardly wait!

This is the first time we've been alone since I met Oriol on the Ramblas. We're walking along the promenade, hand in hand of course, gazing at the fishing boats and the posh yachts. There's not much to say – there never is – but it doesn't matter. There's a comfortable silence between us as we take off our trainers and walk along the beach. I have to say it's not as beautiful as Cornwall. There are no rocks, no surf waves, and the sand isn't as clean as it could be. But right now I couldn't care less about the scenery. We skirt round a group of lads playing football and walk towards the water's edge. Oriol puts his arm around my shoulders, I wrap mine around his waist. He feels warm, familiar. We sit on an abandoned sun-lounger and stare at the calm, still sea. He leans his head close to mine and lets out a contented sigh. Any moment now we're going to kiss – I can feel my lips tingling already!

ALL THE KING'S HORSES
Laura C. Stevenson

It began the day Grandpa escaped . . .

Something very odd has happened to Colin and
Sarah's much-loved grandfather. It's as if a
stranger is inhabiting his body . . . as if Grandpa
has been spirited away and a changeling left in
his place. Raised all their lives on his tales of
great heroes and fantastical legendary
creatures, Colin and Sarah feel sure that the
Faer Folk are involved.

In an attempt to find him again, they follow
Grandpa's path, crossing the boundary between
the everyday world and the enchantments of the
Otherworld . . .

A wonderfully lyrical fantasy adventure
brimming with characters from the Otherworld
– from magnificent horses to mischievous night-
elves and the legendary Sidhe.

ISBN 0 552 54718 2

A CORGI ORIGINAL PAPERBACK

(UN)ARRANGED MARRIAGE
Bali Rai

Harry and Ranjit were waiting for me – waiting to take me to Derby, to a wedding. My wedding. A wedding I hadn't asked for, that I didn't want. To a girl I didn't know . . .

Set partly in the UK and partly in the Punjab region of India, this is a fresh, bitingly perceptive and totally up-to-the-minute look at one man's fight to free himself from family expectations and to be himself, free to dance to his own tune.

ISBN 0 552 54734 4

A CORGI ORIGINAL PAPERBACK

GIRLS UNDER PRESSURE
Jacqueline Wilson

Hi, I'm Ellie. Ellie-Belly. Ellie-phant. That's what I get called by my annoying little brother, Eggs, and even by my best friends, Magda and Nadine. It's because I'm so fat. And I hate it. I'm going on a diet right this minute.

No more strawberry ice cream. No more bacon sandwiches. My step-mother tries to help by saying she'll go on a diet too, but she's skinny already. So is Nadine – so thin she could be a cover girl on a magazine. And Magda's got a perfect figure – she has to fight the boys off (literally, sometimes). They're not being much help, but I'm determined . . .

In this moving and funny sequel to *Girls in Love*, Ellie, Magda and Nadine each try out some drastic changes to their looks but none of it works out quite the way they planned. What should they do? These girls are under pressure . . .

ISBN 0 552 54522 8

A CORGI BOOK